Sweet Gamble

Love Happens • Book Seven

SUSAN WARNER

Sweet Gamble

One

"Why is it that men are only around to open doors and not around to help me carry the heavy pots?"

Daisy Patterson carefully made her way down the steps, aware that one false move could have her tumbling down the ten steps of the courthouse. They were so easy to manage when she had the dolly, and she had brought the plants into the courthouse. When Skye, the owner of the general store, came in to find out if she could borrow a dolly to move some supplies into her store, Daisy volunteered hers.

Her neighborly etiquette might be spot-on, but her long-range thinking needed some work. So here she was paying for her good deed by risking her neck, taking the empty flower pot back to her truck.

"One step at a time," Daisy said, gingerly making it down the steps. If her count was right, she had already made it down four of the ten steps. As if she had invoked Murphy's Law by counting the steps, her foot had to feel for the next one. She could do this like she had done so many times before; she just needed to concentrate and keep her balance.

"Hey, little lady, let me give you a hand," someone said from below her. "I'll help you bring it down."

Daisy blew a hank of her blonde hair out of her face. "I did ask for a man," she muttered. "I didn't really mean it; take him back," she said to no one in particular. Daisy hoped if she just ignored him that maybe he would be offended and go away. She peeked around the large flower pot and saw the shadow of a person climbing the steps toward her.

She pulled in a breath she didn't really have to spare and tried to warn him off. "I'm good," she called out. "Just stay out of my way."

"I'm all for women's liberation, but you need some help," the man replied.

"Nope, been here before, and I know how to do this alone."

Daisy stopped, realizing that when she called out to the stranger, not only did it take away from her strength, but it made the load she carried begin to wobble. The pot was large, and her arms were wrapped around it, basically hugging it close to her chest. In truth, that wasn't the problem. The problem was the bag of dirt inside the pot. Daisy had to keep the pot steady if she wanted to keep the dirt steady so she wouldn't be pushed off balance.

After expending the extra energy and unknowingly shifting the dirt, Daisy shifted the dirt back into the middle of the pot.

"Come on, center yourself already," Daisy said as she leaned to the opposing side, trying to get the dirt back into the center.

"See what I told you? You're already leaning to one side from the weight," the man said from below.

Daisy wondered what would happen if she looked around the pot and just yelled, "Catch!" It would totally serve the guy right, women's liberation and all.

"Thanks," she said. "If you'll just move away from the steps… And don't touch me or I'll lose my balance."

"I'll make sure you're balanced. I've got you."

Then the perfect storm of disaster came. A breeze came by and lifted a hank of Daisy's hair, blinding her. In an attempt to move it, she leaned to one side. Then the man she had been talking to spoke, and he was much closer than she thought. Daisy still couldn't see; when the man spoke, he made her jump in surprise, and whatever balance she had was lost in that instant.

Daisy lost her grip on the pot, and in her attempt to grab it, pitched herself forward. Her hair cleared her face, and as she was falling, she could see the pot rolling down the steps until it hit the bottom, and then it broke into four pieces. She didn't have enough time to moan over the pot because she tried to protect her head as she fell. The next thing she knew, she had slammed into a wall of muscle. She knew it was probably the guy who scared her.

When it was all said and done, at least Mister Interfering had done some good and cushioned her fall. Now all she needed to do is make sure he wasn't hurt. The last thing she needed was a stranger trying to sue her, and they were already on the steps of the courthouse.

Daisy wasn't the one to put off bad news. She pushed herself off of the man, realizing she was bracing herself against a wall of muscle, and thanked her good fortune to fall on one of the last people who actually worked out. She could see he had dark hair and a sturdy body.

He still hadn't listened to her. A person couldn't have it all. He didn't move as she pushed herself up, so she was a little concerned, but his heart felt strong beneath her fingertips and his chest moved up and down in a good rhythm.

"Are you okay?" she asked as she got to her knees and really looked at the man. "Can you move everything or do you need me to—"

Daisy blew an errant strand of blonde hair out of her face to get a better look at her impromptu cushion. She knew this man. Well, not in a neighborly kind of way, but because she had just seen him in the waiting area of the mayor's office. She hadn't given him more than a glance. He was exactly the kind of man she stayed away from. He was tall, with dark hair and beautiful lashes that every woman wanted to have. He had a nice build and probably turned heads wherever he went. On top of all of that, he was dressed in a pair of jeans that looked like they had just come out of the store, and the shirt her hands were on right now had to be the softest shirt she had ever felt on a man. He had all of the signs of a city man.

She'd met a couple of them before. They came to small towns, looked for women who were wowed by their money or worldliness, and then they left. They weren't interested in tomorrow. They weren't interested in building anything. It was true her opinion was probably a bit harsh, but what her mother hadn't taught her she'd learned on her own the hard way.

City men were like candy. In the beginning, it was fun, and you could eat a little, but too much made you sick.

He gave her what must have been his go-to smile.

"Hi," he said. "Now aren't you glad I didn't listen to you and stayed around to help you?"

Daisy rolled her eyes and pushed herself up. "No, I'm not. It would have done us both some good had you been able to follow instructions."

He grinned. "You don't really mean that. I'm Patrick Cunningham by the way," he said as he stood up and brushed off his jeans.

"Well, I'm the owner of the broken pot at the bottom of the steps, and yes, I do wish you had been a little more obedient. Good day!"

"Hold up. I can see you're feeling a little shaken up; let me help you."

Daisy turned to face him and wondered if maybe something had been hurt when she fell on it. "You were the one who just had to mind your business and stay out of the way. You failed to do those simple things that I believe most five-year-olds can do, and now you think you can evaluate my feelings about your ineptitude? Unbelievable!"

"Ineptitude. I can see someone is using S.A.T. words," he said with a grin.

Daisy couldn't really believe he had said that. "Did you really say that? Whatever." She ignored him and went down the steps to look at the damaged pot. As she was looking at the damage, Clarissa came by. Daisy let out a breath and waited. It was going to be a trying day. Clarissa was the town beauty queen. She was a shapely woman who had a razor tongue and was on the town council. Daisy didn't know what she did exactly as work, but when she ran into most people, it wasn't going to be a nice encounter.

"Daisy?"

"Hello, Clarissa."

Clarissa looked behind her. "I don't know who you are, but if this is your way of introducing yourself, you can skip me." Then Clarissa turned back to Daisy. "Do you need help?"

Daisy hoped her mouth wasn't hanging open from the shock of Clarissa being pseudo nice to her. What was the world coming to if Clarissa was being nice?

"I'm good, thank you for asking."

With a nod, Clarissa went on her way. Then, as a rude reminder of why she was on her knees anyway, she looked up to see him standing there. He bent down to try to help her, and she didn't know a way to stop him.

"These shards are big and might cut you. I can throw them away," he offered.

Daisy shook her head. "We don't throw things away here when they get broken. We find another use for them and keep moving."

Patrick stood up. "Okay, what do you want to do with them?"

"You do realize you can go and I'll take care of this?"

"I could, but what kind of person would that make me? I save you, and then I leave you. No, I'll see this through."

"See it through? I think I'd like to see something go through you," Daisy muttered. She stood up and wiped her hands on her jeans.

"Look, my truck is right here. If you can pick up a shard and put it in the back of my truck, that would be helpful."

She watched Patrick flash a smile at her that would have made any other woman want to be best friends with him. Daisy was not moved. When he had finished moving the shards, he came back and smiled at her.

She looked around and then back at him.

"Did you want money?"

His grin became wider. "No, I thought you'd give a thank you."

Daisy looked at him and then let out a sigh of supreme patience.

"You would think that because you're living in a different world. But since I can see that you're not going to leave until you get something, let me say it. Thank you for interfering and breaking my pot. Have a nice day."

With that, Daisy left, shaking her head about how Sweet Blooms was changing and more city people were visiting. She knew it was fashionable to go to the country and see how people roughed it, but she was glad they didn't stay. In fact, during the summer months, she tried to stay away from town because of the increased visits by out-of-towners.

Today's encounter just confirmed all of her thoughts about city folk. Fortunately, it was just a one-time meet up.

Patrick had been waiting for the mayor on the steps of the courthouse just about all day. Nothing had happened since the blonde nymph had left. Patrick had taken up residence on the steps in a diminishing shaft of shade. When the secretary had told him she had called the mayor, he thought it would be, at most, an hour wait. He had been wrong.

Every moment he stayed on the steps looking out at the town, he thought he finally understood what it would be like if the apocalypse hit. Everything in Sweet Blooms was quiet. The cars were quiet. The people on the street were quiet. Patrick had lived in the city all of his life. He didn't think he'd ever been in funeral homes this quiet.

The town was clean, he'd give it that, but the silence was just too much. Finally, he saw the mayor coming up the steps. He knew it was her because she looked just like the picture in her office.

"Ms. Mayor, I'm Patrick Cunningham," he said with a smile. He got that gut feeling that this was not going to go the way he imagined. It was the way she looked down her nose at him, or maybe it was the way she looked him up and down, and then he thought he had somehow come up wanting.

"Hello, Mr. Cunningham, how can I help you?"

Oh yeah, this was not going right at all. She didn't invite him to her office. She didn't offer her hand for a shake. She was giving off all the signs that he was her least favorite person to be talking to right now.

"You received my letters regarding my uncle's inheritance?" he said. He knew she had received them. He had sent them all priority mail.

"Yes I did receive them, but what you want isn't possible."

He looked at her, waiting for her to say, "Joke's on you," but that never happened. He thought he would be in and out of this town the same day. He didn't have enough money to do more than that.

"I'm sorry, Mayor Mason, but I don't understand. Did my uncle leave me the land?"

He saw her shift her weight to one foot in her lavender suit. She let out a breath as if she were about to explain something to a five-year-old and needed patience.

"Your uncle was, indeed, the owner of the land. He

did leave it to you. However, there are trustees of land rules that forbid you to sell it outright."

"What? Listen, I don't want the land. I need the money to get back to my life!"

"I hear you, Mr. Cunningham, but that's not the way it's done in Sweet Blooms."

Panic started to creep over him like a phantom shadow that couldn't be stopped. He hadn't felt this kind of panic since he bet all he had on a bitcoin transaction and lost it all.

"I can get a lawyer, you know. I need the money! Can I get a lien against the land or…or something?"

He saw her jaw tighten before she decided to speak.

"You can, of course, seek counsel, but they will tell you the same. Everyone who has ever owned land here has done it by agreeing to some rules. The first rule is, we can't sell the land to outsiders. The founders of Sweet Blooms believed in preserving history, and the people who came had the same thoughts as well. The second rule is, you can give the land to any member of your family. You don't have to give it to a son or daughter. You can give the land to someone who you think will preserve it and value it. Which, frankly, is why I'm so surprised your uncle gave you the land."

"Listen, my uncle was an odd man. He would talk to me in riddles and tell me I had to come here. When he passed, I was just as surprised as you are that he left me anything. Now that we've both been disappointed, I want to get out of your hair, and you want me gone. Can you tell me how we can do that?"

She gave him a look of exhaustion.

"In the time that I've been Mayor, there has only been one loophole."

"Yes?" He could see her lips were pursed, and she folded her arms over her chest. Obviously, whatever it was she was about to say would be distasteful to everyone.

"There is a caveat that a lien can be put on the land."

Patrick smiled. "Why didn't you say so before?" Patrick was starting to breathe. He kept thinking about the man who currently had his condo and his Benz in lieu of him selling this piece of land. "What do you want me to sign?"

The mayor closed her eyes and shook her head. "It's not that easy. You have to show that you are working the land. You or a relative would also have to be on the land to get the lien."

She gave hope and took it all away in the same breath. He wanted to fall to his knees and curse his uncle for dangling a solution in front of his face and then taking it away. The abject disappointment must have shown on his face.

"Listen, before you make any decisions, I think you should go see the land first," the mayor said.

Patrick wanted to tell her he didn't need to see a pile of dirt to know what it looked like. He wanted to tell her he was leaving tonight and going back to his life, but lady luck hadn't been kind to him. He had taken what he thought was a sure shot on a quick turnover investment into Bitcoin, and then the politics of the world had decided that Bitcoin was bad for three consecutive days. It was unheard of, but he should have known that it would happen when he decided to make some quick cash.

Patrick had already been balancing on a string, and that deal broke it. When the mail came and said he had land, he talked the guys who had come to repossess his condo, which he hadn't paid on in three months, and his leased Mercedes Benz into giving him thirty days. He would then give them the money so he could get his life back.

Then this happened, and now he was down on his luck. His life was like this. He knew he could find a deal and get back on top again if he could only sell this land.

"I'll take a look at the land." The mayor seemed a little more relaxed with that answer.

"Do you have a car?" she asked.

He shook his head no. "Well, I'll take you out there, and when you want to go back to the hotel, call them; I'm sure one of the guys will pick you up."

Patrick nodded. The ride in her car seemed to take forever. With each passing tree, Patrick knew he was falling down a rabbit hole. When she drove up to the one level shack, he stepped out and found his shoes in dust and dirt.

"Mr. Cunningham, take a look around. Remember, when you are ready to go back to the hotel, just give them a call, and they'll come get you."

He watched her drive away; a cloud of dust obscured the view. By the time it settled, her truck was gone.

"Wow, this is a pretty low point, Patty," he said to no one in particular. He walked to the house and turned the knob. It was open. Why did he think otherwise? It looked like something right off one of those TV shows where a man lives in the wild. The place looked clean, considering the location. Patrick found a switch, and when he flicked it, there was light. He was too tired from the day. He would look around in the morning. For now, he saw the couch and laid down.

He'd start trying to figure this out in the morning.

Two

Daisy walked out to the field to check on her herbs. She wasn't supposed to go into town today. She usually tried to schedule one day a week for herself and to check on her crop. The field was about half a mile away from her house. The owner of the land had let her and her mother use this land as long as she could remember.

Daisy remembered coming out to this field with her mother as a child. It was just the two of them, and she taught her everything she knew about herbs and natural medicine. Twice a week they would come to this field, and she'd make sure Daisy could identify and recite every herb and flower she saw. A smile touched Daisy's lips as she recalled her making teas and tinctures and her mother smiling when she got it right and patiently reviewing it when she got it wrong.

Daisy could talk about any subject with her mother except one: her father. The only thing her mother would say was the past had to stay in the past; she couldn't fix what she couldn't find.

As her mind wandered, she walked through the rows, checking her basil and peppermint for any spots, holes, or signs of their deteriorating health when she heard him.

"Hello?!"

She stood up and looked at the man approaching her. It was him, the city-dweller. Why was he here? As he came closer, she could see that he had a five o'clock shadow and he was in the same clothes he had on yesterday. She started walking towards him, wondering what was he doing out here.

"I'm so glad I found you," he said, out of breath.

She watched him come closer to her and became aware of how isolated they were. She slowly bent down and picked up her basket as she pasted a smile on her face. As he came closer, panting out of breath, she reached in and grabbed the end of her trowel.

"Oh, thank goodness! A face I know!" he said, gasping.

"I don't think we know each other, and I have to ask you what you're doing out here," she said as he bent over at the waist and tried to get his breath back. Holding up his hand, he motioned for her to give him a moment.

"The mayor brought me out here, and I thought she was coming back out to get me, but she was tied up. I tried to call the hotel to come and get me, and they said they only do pickups in the morning. I tried to explain to him that's why I was calling him."

Daisy heard his out of breath explanation. "It's true, they do pickups in the morning. It's already ten-thirty, so you've missed the morning pickups."

He stood up and ran a hand through his dark hair.

"That's what he said to me."

Daisy tightened her grip on the rubber handle. "Look, Mr.—"

He interrupted her, wiped his hand on his pants, and then held out his hand in greeting.

"It's Mr. Patrick Cunningham."

"Cunningham?"

"Yes."

"As in a relation of old man Cunningham?" she asked. This just couldn't be. If this man was the relative Carl Cunningham spoke of, then this situation had just gone from bad to worse.

"Yeah, that was my uncle," Patrick said with a smile.

She didn't take his hand. She looked at it and him and just couldn't believe how bad her luck was. She harrumphed and then shook her head.

"Good day to you, Mr. Cunningham." She didn't say good-bye; she just turned and started home. The afternoon sun was beginning to climb, and she could feel the heat starting to build. There was an underwater tube in all five rows of her meager plot. The only thing Daisy could think about was where she would move her little plot. She knew the city guy would try to sell the place or rent it to the real estate person. That's what city people did. They came in and found something or someone of value, and then they sold it or them. It would take about a month before she could harvest her plants. She should have enough time if he tried on his own.

"Hey, hey, hold up. I need your help," he cried out. She could hear him running behind her, and she turned to see him standing on one of her basil plants. Behind him, she could see he had trampled three other plants.

It was the last straw when she looked at him; all she saw was destruction and heartache. She dropped her basket and headed towards him with her trowel in hand.

At first, he smiled, and she could tell the moment he saw her approaching him with intent. He held his hands out in front of him.

"Hold up there. I don't know what you're thinking, but I just needed a ride."

He took a step back, and she called out. "Stop moving! You're stepping on my basil."

"Basil?"

"Yes! It's the green plants you are stepping on!"

He looked down and then looked up at her and the trowel. "I thought it was just grass."

Daisy rolled her eyes. "Why am I not surprised? Walk in a line and follow me. I'll take you into town."

With exaggerated steps, he followed Daisy. She looked over her shoulder every five steps and tried not to be extremely annoyed by his presence. She kept her hearing alert to his trudging behind her.

"What were you before, a ballerina? I don't know how you get so quickly through these rows."

She wanted to call back over her shoulder that the trick she knew was how to walk in a straight line. She didn't want him here. She couldn't believe her life was in his hands, but it was. She kept thinking about where she could move her garden. Both this year's and next year's crops were already in the ground. Would he tell her to leave without getting her harvest for the year?

She needed to be nice to him if for no other reason than he was related to Mr. Cunningham. Not to mention that until she could explain how and why she was on his land, she was going to have to work with him.

She was so deep in thought that she almost missed hearing his steps behind her. She turned to see what he was doing. He was looking down at his feet, making sure he stayed in the row. If the situation wasn't so serious, she would have laughed. He looked like a child trying to put one foot in front of the other.

On top of that, she could see the sweat pouring down his face.

"Why were you at the Cunningham place?"

"I told you—"

"No, why did you stay and not go back to where you feel more comfortable?" she asked. She hoped it sounded concerned and not pushy.

"I wanted to, believe me, but selling this land isn't as easy as it seems," he said while trying to catch his breath. Daisy heard the deep breaths and had to look over her shoulder more than once to make sure he wasn't about to pass out.

"You wanted to sell the land?" she reiterated. All the while, in the back of her mind, she was telling herself why she now knew he was crazy. The land was so rich that he'd make more money renting it out to people than selling it outright.

"I need to sell this land. I owe a lot of money, and I know my uncle understood that I needed to live in the city. That is why I don't understand why it's so hard for me to sell it."

He sounded confused and perplexed. It took everything in Daisy not to become hysterical at the nonchalant way he was discounting her life. Sell the land? Who would ever sell the land for city life? She knew she had called it right when she called him a city dweller. They didn't understand the relationship between people and the land.

"So what's holding you up?" she asked.

"Would you believe a bunch of dead people?"

"What?"

"The mayor keeps telling me about rules; about the founding fathers and how the land is held in trust; about how the only way out is to make sure I work the land.

It's just foolishness. This is the 21st century. I want my money, and I want to leave here."

"And what you have in the city is so amazing that it made you come here to sell off what you had of your history?" she asked.

"Well, it's hard to explain what I have in the city." They were finally out of her field and now on a dirt road. She turned to look at him. "I made a bad investment in the city, so I'm not living in the way I should be, but I know I can get it back.

She'd seen television shows about people like him. The guy who just needed one more opportunity.

When she nodded her head in understanding, he grinned. "I'm going to invest in stocks little by little, so I won't have so much at risk."

"Are you going to be working?"

His grin faded away. "Day trading is working."

She turned and continued to walk towards the car. "I think you will find that it will be a hard sell to explain to the board or to the mayor."

"I hope you're wrong because that is my best pitch. Give me my land so I can get out of your hair and go live my life."

As they walked side by side, his shadow covered hers. He was taller than her and broader in the shoulder. His was probably a gym body. If he had been any other person visiting Sweet Blooms, she might have given him a second look.

"Have you ever lived in any other place than a city?"

"Nope."

"Well then, working with Sweet Blooms' version of red tape should be interesting. It's more about feelings and less about the law."

He shrugged. "It doesn't matter. Bureaucracy is bureaucracy. I'll talk to them, and hopefully it won't cost me too much of the property value."

She gave him another glance as they walked towards her truck. She could imagine his attractive features had made his life a little easier. He looked too put together, too smooth. A man born with that many cards in his favor wouldn't be for her. Daisy dreamed of a man who understood a day's work. Preferably, she wanted a farmer. A person who would love the land like she did.

"This is the second time I've seen you, but I'm not sure what you do," he said.

"I run the floral shop and offer organic herbs."

"Is there a market for that here? I would think with everyone owning a farm or living on a farm there wouldn't be one."

Daisy smiled. "It's true, they could try to grow their own items, but no one has as much patience as they once did. If people are on farms, very few are working farms, so it all works out."

"Well, it seems like you have a nice gig here. I'm glad someone found a niche here. I just want to take care of my business and be on my way."

"It's probably for the best."

"The best?"

"Yes, you don't seem like you'd be the type of person to fit in with Sweet Blooms. You are so *go-go-go* and all."

"Well, I don't think I'd want to fit in with this laid back atmosphere."

There was a pregnant silence, and then they were at the car. She opened the door and then gave him the keys.

"What are you doing?"

She smiled at him and then shook her head. "Making a point and helping you out all at once."

"Well, it looks like you just gave me your truck."

"No, I'm letting you drive my truck into town. Leave it in town, and later on, I'll pick it up. I have someone coming to pick me up later today."

Patrick smiled. "How do you know that I'll bring it back?"

She shook her head and looked at him. "That fact that you have to ask that question tells me you might not be a fit for around here."

Patrick palmed the keys and then looked around. "You're probably right. I'm probably not the right kind of person for Sweet Blooms."

"It's always better when people come to these realizations on their own."

With that, he got into the car and then drove off. She watched him and her truck go down the wrong way and make the wrong turn. She almost felt sorry for him but then realized it was better for him to figure out how things were in Sweet Blooms.

Three

Patrick had shown up at the mayor's office. She hadn't been happy to see him. All the time he had been listening to her talk about how it was inappropriate to see the board without being on the schedule, he kept hearing Daisy's words in his head. He didn't fit in.

He didn't know why he was so moved when she said those words; he'd been hearing those words all of his life. His mother loved Uncle Carl. He grew up between the city and the country. He could have told Daisy that it might have changed her mind, but he hadn't. He had been unprepared to hear the words from such a pretty face.

He nodded his head appropriately when the mayor spoke and thought about leaving this town as soon as he could.

"So you see that meeting the board would be your only chance to sell, and according to the guidelines, you'd have to accept whatever the board came up with."

Patrick plastered on his best boy scout smile. He had been wheeling and dealing in the city for years. He couldn't see a small town giving him any trouble. With an understanding look, he scooted forward in the chair and placed his hand on the mayor's desk.

"I understand what you're saying, and I'm confident that we'll all be able to come to an agreement that works for us all." Patrick could see the mayor looked less than convinced, but he was confident in his ability to work a room. Eventually, she capitulated and told him to come back to the chamber in an hour. He took that hour to pull himself together and go over some points of the speech. He had gotten a list of names, ages, and ethnicities. He knew he could do this.

Patrick was feeling prepared until he walked into the room. The mayor had told him they would meet in the chamber. When he went inside that "chamber," he found it was really more of a room. The dais where the board members were sitting was nothing more than a raised platform, and the board members looked like a collection of people from a grab bag. None of them wore suits. One of the women there he had seen before in passing, and she appeared to be the youngest person on the board.

He looked at the hodgepodge and realized he'd never had to deal with people who weren't city officials or politicians. His speeches had been crafted for those who wanted a political career or in the very least wanted to stay elected. Not one to back down, he walked into the chamber and sat down at the oblong table and looked up at the board.

The mayor got it all started with a banging of her hand on the table.

"Patrick Cunningham asked for an emergency meeting. He's—"

"There ain't no need to tell me his name. The boy looks just like Carl. I'm Jerry, by the way. Carl and I were friends."

Patrick nodded. "Thank you, Jerry. I'm grateful that you all gathered so that I could—"

"I'm Agnes, and you talk too fast. You remind me of a car salesman who knows the car will drop dead any moment."

Patrick turned to the older woman sitting next to Jerry. Just when he was about to say something, he was cut off again. This time by a beautiful woman who he didn't mind at all.

"Now, now, everyone, let's hear what Patrick Cunningham has to say. If for no other reason than we all knew his uncle, Carl."

"To whom do I have the pleasure of thanking?" he said smoothly.

Agnes snorted. "I know he's full of it now, and he's stupid to fall for some pretty words from Clarissa."

The mayor cleared her throat. "Everyone, please, I want you to wait and listen to what Patrick has come to ask." When it looked as if they all nodded, the mayor looked at Patrick to take the floor.

"For all of you who don't know, let me introduce myself again to you all. My name is Patrick Cunningham. My uncle was Carl Cunningham, and he left a large plot of land that resides here in Sweet Blooms." He looked around the room to assess the crowd's reaction. So far, they all looked like someone had served prunes and told them it was raisins.

"I always knew Carl was too sentimental," said one of the members. "He always thought Sweet Blooms could heal all people. He didn't understand the younger generation was just lost."

The mayor looked to her side and gave a stern look down the table. "It is not the opinion of everyone at this table that the younger generation is lost, Jerry. I will agree that Carl was often hasty about decisions and had to have them fixed later," she said, and then turned her gaze back on Patrick.

Patrick squirmed under her gaze. Clearing his throat, he paused for an opportunity to jump in and try to turn the tide.

"Obviously, all of you knew my uncle on a daily basis. I wasn't as fortunate because I built my life in the city. While we kept in touch, I can't claim the closeness that I'm sure all of you had with him. As a result, this gift he left me was unexpected. I have a life back in the city and, to be truthful, I'd like to get back to it. What I'm asking from the board is this: if I can just sell my land back to the town, or to whomever you choose, for a fair price."

"To put this into context for the board members, let me remind you that after speaking with our counsel," the mayor continued. "Land is held in trust. All the land is to stay with Sweet Blooms, and no one person can sell a parcel of land. They could relinquish, or the town can buy it back."

"Well, it sounds pretty simple to me; he just needs to give the land back," Agnes announced.

It took all of Patrick's training not to drop his jaw at the comment. He looked up and down the table, and none of them seemed to see why that solution wasn't feasible.

"It seems as though Mr. Cunningham isn't looking to give the land back. He's looking to get money in exchange for the land."

"So he's here for the money? What did I tell you about the younger generation? They are lost. Don't understand tradition or—"

The mayor held up her hand, interrupting Jerry's tirade. "The other caveat is that the bylaws state he can't sell the land, and the town doesn't have to buy back the land unless he can show that he has worked the land and wasn't able to match his income or make the land profitable at all."

Patrick interjected. "Please listen. I'm not trying to collect a fortune here. I just want a fair offer, and then I'll leave. You can have your land back."

The council members looked at one another, and then Agnes spoke.

"Well, I guess it's good that you just want to get your cash and go. But I'm going to have to agree with Jerry. It's the young generation that gets too much for nothing. You want your money. I'm all for buying the land after you've worked it; otherwise, tough kitties," she said as she sat back in her chair and crossed her arms over her chest.

"You know, I read somewhere that if we put the younger generation back into the situations we went through, they could learn some backbone and conscious." Jerry shrugged.

Patrick watched the mayor look at the other members and nod her head. This discussion was going south faster than he could control it.

The mayor looked over at him, then at the paper in front of her, and then she lifted her gaze to Patrick once more.

"Mr. Cunningham, if you would like to say something, you can. I want to make sure that everyone hears your voice and your opinion."

Patrick heard her but thought she couldn't be serious. He looked at the board, and if it were possible, he knew they'd all put him in front of a firing squad for every young person they thought they knew.

"I just want to say that I want to do what is best for the town. It's not my intention to auction the land or do anything that would interfere with the town morals or land trust. In fact, I believe that it is best if I just exchange the land for its value back to the town."

Clarissa began to clap her hands, and it stopped his speech cold. He looked over at the attractive woman and for once really took note of more than just her physical assets, which were obvious; this time, he also took the time to look into her intelligent brown eyes. She had a smile that looked as if it belonged to the Cheshire cat, and she folded her hands and rested her head on them.

"Well, then, Mr. Cunningham, this should be a rather painless exchange. I am so glad that you said you are interested in our morals and upholding the land trust. By doing those two things, Sweet Blooms has been able to prosper more in the last eight months than it has been able to do in the last five years. Hearing your commitment to our ways, I think the path is clear, wouldn't you say, Mayor?"

Patrick did a double take and saw the smile on the mayor's face widen.

"I believe that Clarissa is right. My judgment is this. Come back in a year and let's see how the situation is."

"A year—" sputtered Patrick. "I don't have a year. I can't put my life on hold for a year."

Jerry shook his head. "The younger generation is so impatient; so glad that missed my boy."

Agnes chimed in. "The boy looks lost. I'm willing to cut him some slack. How about he comes back in a month and we'll see how he's doing then. I mean, you know the saying—if you're going to fail, then fail fast."

Mayor nodded along with Agnes and then turned to Patrick.

"After review, you can come back in a month, and we'll make a decision then. During that time, you will have to fulfill the mandate and work the land."

Patrick looked around and saw no faces that would help him fight this. He had to nod his head and paste on a smile. "Thank you."

They all got up, but not before Patrick heard Agnes say, "That boy's smile was so fast, I thought his face was going to crack. Young'ins."

Four

Patrick walked to the hotel, and he was tired and sticky. He wasn't sure if he was going to pack his bags and leave or just reflect on the incredulous morning. When he had finished taking his shower, he realized as much as he might want to, going back home wasn't an option. He had to think, and giving up wasn't on the table.

He went down to the lobby and asked if he could get a lift. The front desk clerk said yes. When he got into the car, the young man looked in the rearview mirror, waiting for Patrick to give him a destination. Without hesitation, he told him to the Cunningham place. When the young man seemed like he wasn't going to drive, Patrick asked him if he knew where it was. If he didn't, it wasn't like he was going to be able to tell him either. Fortunately, he did and began to drive.

Patrick understood negotiations. He understood the world was full of give and take situations. He had been looking for the big deal that would end all deals all of his life, but he hadn't found it. Instead, he'd been a day late and a dollar short to the big windfalls. He knew bitcoin was going to be big; he could even live off the volatility if he could just get enough capital to matter.

He'd been told most of his life he was a risk-taker, that he was too close to the end, but the one thing he always remembered growing up was hearing his mother tell him that a bad apple comes from a bad seed. Patrick hadn't known his father. He was determined to show his family otherwise. It's not like he'd been a complete loser. He'd made thousands and then reinvested in things and lost those thousands. He didn't mind the loss. His thought was if he could do it once, he could do it again. The problem always seemed to be having enough capital to move. When he had received word on this property, he thought those woes were gone. Again, it looked like he had counted his chickens before they hatched, as his uncle would have said.

"The middle of nowhere," he muttered under his breath, letting the reality of the surroundings sink in. All he saw out the window as it went by were trees and land. He wanted to yell and say *wake up*, in the hopes it was just a horrible dream.

Finally, the car pulled up to the property in front of the house. He got out and watched the car leave. He was alone. On a property that he had no idea what to do with. After the meeting, the mayor had gone over the basics. He couldn't do nothing. He had to show some effort. Effort sounded like money. Money he didn't have. He started walking, looking around the property. At this rate, the kindest thing that could happen would be for a bear to come by and eat him. The land was so flat that he could see clear across it. In the distance, he thought he saw something shimmer, and when he took another look, he could see it again. He walked towards it.

He knew it was Daisy. Daisy. Being so deep in his woes, he'd forgotten about Daisy. Why was she here?

And wasn't this Cunningham land? Maybe he could talk to her about what could be done on the land. Their last meeting wasn't something he'd write home about, but maybe he'd get a break since it seemed like she was with someone.

He knew he was sweating by the time he got to them. He had opened up a button on his shirt, and his feet were feeling hot in his loafers. He put all of that aside and walked slowly as to not startle the women. As he approached them, he could see the other woman had dark hair, and she was laughing.

The women seemed as though they were collecting herbs from the ground. Each one had what appeared to be a small basket and in them lay what he could only quantify as dead plants. He knew his way around a floral shop. He could pick out a rose from a carnation, but these all looked like weeds. Patrick could see the sun reflecting off of Daisy's wavy hair. She was fit and attractive. In fact, he knew if they had met in any other place, she would have been the woman for him. However, she was a Sweet Blooms resident, and that meant she was a lifer kind of woman. Right now, Patrick was all about making his money and hitting it big. Daisy might be a way to get that.

The other woman spotted him, and Daisy turned to see him as well. He couldn't see her expression, but he went forward to greet the woman.

"You must be Patrick Cunningham, the one everyone is talking about," she said, holding out her hand. She held the basket in her other hand. "I'm Hannah Jenkins. Nice to meet you."

"Soon to be Hannah Cade," interjected Daisy with a smile.

Hannah smiled and nodded. Patrick shook her hand and nodded back.

Hannah was an attractive woman. She must have been in her late thirties, with a ready smile, dark hair, and she had a way about her that made a person feel comfy.

"So, the rumor is the board denied you the right to sell until you can show if you can tough it out," Hannah said.

"Wow, word travels quickly. I just got back here to look over what I have to work with."

Daisy turned to him and looked as if she had just been sideswiped.

"You're staying?" Daisy asked.

Patrick smiled. "At least everyone doesn't know. Yes, it looks that way. I wanted to talk to you about that."

Hannah looked between the two of them.

"Well, it's definitely time for me to go. Daisy, thank you for the bundle. Charge it to my account, and I'll see you in the shop later this week to settle up," Hannah said as she walked away.

Patrick waved at Hannah's retreating figure. "It's nice to meet you, Ms. Jenkins."

"Please, it's Hannah. By the time you get used to Jenkins, I'll be a Cade. We're informal out here, Patrick, as I'm sure you'll discover."

Daisy watched Hannah go and tried to gather the words she would say to Patrick. She had heard the news about Patrick's situation, and the only thing she could think about was how this going to affect her. She was kicking herself for not taking any paper from Cunningham. He had offered her a paper about the plot of land she used, but she didn't want to offend him.

Patrick, on the other hand, was a totally different issue. She knew he wasn't happy to be here; he wanted to do whatever he could to put Sweet Blooms behind him. Daisy knew life didn't always give you what you wanted. She'd learned that lesson as the daughter of a single mother in Sweet Blooms. The people in Sweet Blooms loved her mother, and they embraced her when she opened the floral shop. Daisy grew up with people's well-meaning pity. Daisy worked hard to have to ask for nothing, and the only time she broke that rule was for this plot on Carl Cunningham's land. Carl had met her mother, and the two of them had been kindred souls. Both of them had love and lost. They weren't looking for another love; they just wanted to live in peace.

Daisy knew she had been her mother's whole focus in life. The agreement to use the land had been there before she was born and never questioned since. Would Patrick let her stay? What did he plan to do on the land?

Hoping and wishing wasn't going to answer those questions. There was only one way to find out. She was going to have to talk to him and ask the questions.

Daisy turned to Patrick and saw him waiting for her to say something to break the silence.

"I've got work to be done, but my place is within walking distance of here. Do you have a car?"

"No."

She wanted to roll her eyes and scream at his lack of being prepared, or maybe he thought people were supposed to chauffeur him around. Taking a deep breath, she let it out.

"Follow me."

She walked to the end of the row until they were on the dirt path.

"Follow this path for twenty minutes. It leads up to my house. I have to finish some invoices and calls, but after that, we can talk things through. I'll see you in about an hour?"

Patrick smiled. "You got yourself a date."

Daisy nodded and turned away. A date, he said. He wished it was a date. At this rate, it was going to take all of her composure and manners to be civil to him.

Thirty minutes had passed, and already, he was a problem. After twenty minutes, she heard a disturbance of the birds outside her window. When she got up from her desk and looked out the window in her study, she saw him sitting in the front yard. Frustration made her turn away from the window and sit down at her desk to complete the invoices she had to do for that afternoon. After signing ten more invoices, she peeked out the window again to see if he was still there, and sure enough, he was outside now pacing back and forth in the yard. Taking a deep breath, she gave up all hope of trying to do the rest of her work for the afternoon and went to the door to try to deal with the problem that was Patrick.

When she opened up her door, he stopped pacing and gave her his full attention. He looked out of place in her front yard, just like he looked out of place in Sweet Blooms. Daisy had to admit the thing that irked her the most about him was his smile. It was perfect. It was perfectly fake. He reminded her one of those models in a commercial where you could never tell what they were selling. She became frustrated with herself when she unconsciously ran her hands over her hair. What did it matter if her hair was in place? Would he even notice that she had put on clean jeans and had on a rose top?

This man took her orderly thinking and turned it upside down. The best thing that she could possibly do now would be to find out how they could help each other and then go their separate ways.

"Are you ready for me?" he asked.

"Any time," she countered, then she closed her door behind her and offered him a seat on the bench in front of her house.

"I thought we'd go inside where it would be cooler," Patrick said.

Daisy smiled. "It's cooler out here than in my house. Besides, this isn't a social call. I'm not clear what it is yet, so I'd prefer to sit outside."

She saw his smile tighten, and then he gestured for her to sit first. She was taken aback for a moment by his politeness, but then she nodded and took a seat. When he sat down next to her on the bench, it was as if all of the space had been picking up. Patrick Cunningham, what a large man. As Daisy sat next to him, she couldn't remember the last time she had sat next to a man on this bench.

They faced one another on the bench, and the cool wind riffled through his dark hair.

"So, you saw the board today, and they gave you an answer," she started.

"They didn't give me an answer; they gave me an impossible task. I told them I didn't want to stay. I told them I would leave if they just gave me a fair price."

Daisy smiled. "I can see how that might not have gone over very well. You might think a town wants money, but the town of Sweet Blooms is a different animal."

"I thought they'd be happy to see me go. But I have to tell you, by the time we had finished the meeting, I felt like they were more interested in seeing how I'd make a fool of myself."

Daisy sighed. "Unfortunately, that sounds like Jerry and Agnes. If you listen to them long enough, you'll hear their thoughts on the younger generation."

"I did, and I have to tell you it's been a long time since someone called me a part of the younger generation. I didn't think there would be a whole lot of wrangling here. Facing them was like being in one of my meetings, and I wasn't expecting a scene like that here in Sweet Blooms."

Daisy gave him a second look. "Here in Sweet Blooms, you have to remember we all look at you like you're a city person. I mean, there's nothing wrong with the city, but the first thing they hear coming out of your mouth when you find out you have land from your family is 'how much will you give me for it?'"

She saw his hand clench. "I get that it may seem a bit cold to everyone here, but this isn't my home."

"You know, Patrick, you don't seem like you really have a home. For people who value family, it makes it hard to deal with you."

"I'm doing the best I can to get my life together. It's true, I don't have a house that ninety generations were born in, but I would like to rebuild my life."

"To us, for you not to have a steady life is odd. It's a weird kind of litmus test. We want to help those we can find common ground with. You want to throw away the thing we have in common. I'm sure that's one of the reasons the board gave you those conditions. I don't think it's about you staying but them being able to find common ground."

Patrick leaned back on the bench and looked out at her yard. She heard him let out a breath. "You're right. Finding common ground is step one in any negotiation."

"I'm glad I could help you."

"Speaking about common ground, am I right in thinking your garden is on Cunningham land?"

Daisy heard the question, but still, it took the wind out of her. She knew it would come up, but still, hearing the words out loud made it all so much more immediate and real.

"Yes, I'm on Cunningham land."

"I'm not looking to kick you off the land or charge you anything. I just need to get an understanding of all of the pieces that are working here."

"Okay. Your uncle let my mother have the land to grow her herbs. I run the floral shop, and I get shipments for flowers, but the herbs and tinctures I grow myself and sell."

"Did your family grow herbs?"

"You should know because, eventually, someone will say it. My mom arrived in Sweet Blooms, pregnant. She and Carl got along well enough. He let her use the land. They were never involved, but they had a friendship that worked for them."

"You were fortunate to have someone who left you something useful."

"I'll trade facts with you, Patrick."

He looked at her. "Common ground?"

She smiled. "Common ground."

"You go first," he said.

Daisy looked around her front yard and tried to reach for just one thing to share.

"It was just the two of us, but my mom was amazing, intelligent, and funny," she said. "She was also a free spirit who would try anything once." Daisy turned to face Patrick on the bench. "We built this bench. You wouldn't know it, but it's bench number four. The other three editions didn't make the final cut and wound up as firewood," she said with a laugh.

"My mom was always worried about me. We lived alone. Our family, such that we have, is spread across the United States. She was the oldest of three. She never spoke much about my father except to say the best thing he ever did was marry her and leave."

Daisy heard the story and couldn't imagine the kind of home he described. He looked at her and shook his head.

"Sorry, we were supposed to be sharing common ground, not spilling our drama."

"No, it's fine. I'm happy to hear if you want to share."

She looked at Patrick and thought he had it all. That he had come from the city and he was just not the right kind. After hearing his story, she was more than grateful for the people in Sweet Blooms and her mother. Daisy had a lot of complaints, but never did she doubt that her mother loved her and was totally devoted to her. She also never doubted that if she needed to, she could go to any person in Sweet Blooms and get help. Patrick seemed like he had been alone for a long time.

Patrick gave a wry laugh. "Part of the reason I wanted the money was because I want to be able to build a home one day. I want to have something stable. I think we all want to do that," Patrick said. "I know I'm getting older, and being old, alone, and poor is not a good look."

Daisy smiled at him. "Older? You aren't even in your late forties yet. The way science is going, the average life expectancy has upped to 100. What that means for you is you're nowhere near midlife."

"Time may fly when you are having fun, but it crawls when you think there's no movement in your life and you're going in circles."

Daisy took a moment to really look at him. His eyes were dark, intent, and framed by long, spiky lashes many a woman would kill for. His shoulders were wide, and overall, he was an attractive man.

"Okay, you are facing the end of times and you're stuck with the board's ultimatum; what is it that you want to do?"

"I'd appreciate it if you could help me look over the land and maybe come up with some ideas on how to satisfy the board but not go broke."

She nodded. They both stood up and walked to the dirt road that led back to his place.

"I'm going to get going, or it'll be on the front page that the new Cunningham owner had to be found in the dark."

She wanted to tell him it wasn't that bad, but when she thought about some of the characters in Sweet Blooms, she couldn't with a straight face. Then he reached out and gave her a quick hug.

"Thanks."

Daisy didn't move. Instead, she watched him walk away until he made the turn in the road as if she were some lovesick teenager. It couldn't be. It couldn't be that every eligible male in Sweet Blooms had asked her out or taken her on a date and nothing had stirred in her but this city dweller, only in town for a minute, would be the one to make her insides quiver. She shook her head. It was just that he was different, that was it. This would pass. She would not be attracted to Patrick Cunningham. She would not be attracted to the only man who couldn't wait to get out of Sweet Blooms.

Five

The bell rang over the door to the floral shop. Daisy didn't bother to look up. She could tell from the smell of jasmine brought in by the breeze that it was Hannah.

"Good morning, Hannah."

"Oh, is it? I wasn't sure after I left you yesterday with Mr. Cunningham."

Daisy stopped arranging the delicate baby breath's stalks and spied Hannah with a Cheshire cat look on her face.

"I spoke with Mr. Cunningham. You know I'm on his land, and I wanted to know what he was going to do. As it stands, he doesn't know what he's going to do or when. He is so focused on getting back to the city that he never considered a monkey wrench like the one the council threw at him."

Hannah waved that off and then leaned on the counter, looking into Daisy's eyes.

"That was good enough fodder, but what I really want to know is what is going on with you and Patrick?"

Daisy gave Hannah her full attention. "Nothing. Why would you even ask?"

"First, your whole body tensed when he spoke. He had a smile on his face that made me unsure if he was pained or a shark about to take a bite. This thing is, the both of you are working together when I know you have a special place in your heart for city folks and you invited him over to your place instead of just having a conversation with him in the field like you would most people you don't particularly care for."

Daisy put her hand on her chest and gave an outraged look. "One, I didn't know you were so observant, and two, what kind of woman do you think I am to date the man whose land I'm staying on?" Unable to hold her composure any longer, Daisy laughed and shook her head at Hannah.

"It's true, I spoke to him, but I'm not running down the aisle to be married. We may be friends at best. I don't think he's the enemy. I was a bit hasty to drop him in the bag with all the city folks. I can change my mind, okay?"

Hannah picked up a sprig of baby's breath and inhaled.

"That is definitely different."

"I don't have to be the same all the time."

"So you're trying to say you may like this person?"

Daisy smiled. "I don't think he's about to bring the wrath of evil down upon me, no."

"Would you agree he may be pleasant to look at?"

"I agree he's not ugly."

Hannah laughed. "So I guess we wouldn't have to put a paper bag over his head if we went out with him?"

Daisy's hands flew to her mouth to hold in the laughter. "You've got to stop. He doesn't need a bag. He probably wouldn't even understand the point if you gave him one. I would go so far as to say he might be considered eye candy."

Hannah stood up and grinned.

"You do think he's hot!"

Daisy groaned and looked around her empty shop. "Don't even say it jokingly. You know the rash of relationships that have been going on now that we're working on the town. I don't want to be part of the gossip."

Hannah stood with her arms folded, waiting.

Daisy threw up her hands. "Alright, alright," Daisy said grudgingly. "He's someone I wouldn't mind walking down Main Street with, but it's just curiosity. He's a fish out of water here in Sweet Blooms, and I couldn't survive in the bustle of the city. To me, it just means that I'm a healthy adult woman."

"Yes, you are. In fact, I've been trying to get you to remember you are a woman for forever."

"I heard you, now we can drop it?"

Hannah held her hands up and went to the door. When she pulled open the door, she looked over her shoulder.

"I'll come to check on my order later because I was totally distracted by the morning conversation. Also, I just thought I'd mention, blondes are so in this time of year."

Daisy couldn't respond because Hannah had already left the shop; the only thing Daisy heard was her laughing down the street.

Blondes are in? Good to know, thought Daisy, but it didn't matter. She wasn't fishing.

"I thought it would be darker," Patrick said, looking around the floral shop.

"It seems contradictory to have a shop where you can't see the flowers," Daisy said as Patrick walked into her shop. "The goal is for everyone to see into all of the corners; that way, they can pick which flowers they want in their arrangements or maybe even buy something that is already pre-done."

"So that glimpse of you frolicking through the fields holding your basket up high and cutting down herbs to create miracle cures, not happening?"

"For so many reasons, that is never going to happen. You are obviously watching entirely too much television."

"I don't know, you have the whole blonde thing going on. I was thinking maybe you were a mix of Mary Poppins, Glenda the Good Witch, and the woman on the hill archetype."

She grinned at him and shook her head. "I gave in the wand last year—insurance, you know, the whole flying thing, couldn't get my license—and the woman on the hill archetype has been retired for a bit." She beckoned him to enter the store instead of blocking the doorway. "The store is narrow, but there is more in the back."

Patrick followed her down the hallway to the back of the store. He was glad she had made time for him. He hadn't called. He had just gotten a car rental for a few days, and he had the need to show it off to someone. It wasn't a great car; in fact, he realized that if he had been anywhere else but Sweet Blooms, he might have been offended to drive it, but it was a sturdy third hand-me-down that he could afford. It was a stick shift, which took a minute for him to remember how to operate, but eventually, it came back to him.

When he had driven a couple of miles in a circle, he realized he wanted to share this with someone. Before he had actually registered the thought as a plan, he pulled over and asked where the floral shop was. The person shook her head and pointed down the main street.

"It's the last shop on the lane. If you take the main street out of Sweet Blooms, you can't help but see it."

It took him a little longer than he thought to get there, but the woman hadn't lied; it was indeed the last shop on the lane. He drove by the shops on Main, then he went by the houses on the block, and then there were two empty lots and the floral shop. It was the last breath of fresh air you'd see before leaving the town of Sweet Blooms.

He hadn't even told her about the car yet. He would tell her when the time was right. Right now, he had an urge to learn as much as he could about Daisy. She'd already explained to him that a majority of the requests that came in for flowers had to do with thanks and congratulations. The town was so small that when someone passed, everyone knew, and she donated the floral arrangements to the funeral for free.

"Don't you think you miss out on a lot of income when you do that?" he asked.

"People in Sweet Blooms are long-lived, so the first answer would be no, I don't. And here on the counter, all by itself with no other partners to share, is my coffee machine. It has a place of honor because I use it faithfully three times a day. You are, fortunately, just in time for one of those occasions."

After watching her grind beans, attach a contraption to the spout, and then pour only pure water into it, fifteen minutes later, they had coffee. He could feel Daisy's stare on him.

"Go ahead and ask; I'm better prepared," he said.

"Did you decide on anything?"

"Well, today I rented what must be a third-hand rental. So I guess I've made a decision to give it a shot. I have a little bit of money, and we'll see how far that gets me."

She nodded and took another sip of her coffee. "I think if you had said this when we first met, I would have blown you off. I know how hard it is to want something and have to go through hoops to get it. It took a lot for the town to give this land to my mom when she wanted to open the shop. It was free for the first six months and then she made enough to pay for it. But she always told me those first six months were the hardest. She would sell flowers by going into town and delivering them to places every day. She told me she worked sun up to sun down."

"I don't mind working. It's when you have to work, and then you lose it all, or it just seems to slip away."

Daisy cocked her head to the side, and he watched as a curtain of her hair rested on her shoulder.

"You know there are no guarantees. If you are waiting for the big one, then maybe you should reconsider this venture."

Patrick smiled. "Well, I've already told all of my creditors and people that I had arrangements with that I'd be gone for sixty days, so going back is really not an option."

"You have people watching your things?"

Patrick inhaled the aroma of his coffee and took a sip. "I took a risk, but it didn't work out. So there aren't many things I have that aren't in hock or in some sort of holding. I tell you that because I have found when you are in these situations, you don't have as many friends or people who will help you out."

Daisy's forehead scrunched up as he saw her try to understand his situation.

"You don't have people who will help you in a bind?"

"I've had people who have helped me in the past, but let's just say they don't understand my vision and they want to help me but only when they approve of my actions. I'm more visionary and impulsive."

He didn't know a better way to explain it because he hadn't come to terms with it either. He could find lots of good investment ideas. In fact, a lot of his "friends" had made a lot of money from his investment ideas. When it came time to float him some money, they weren't as open or willing to listen.

He was almost thirty-eight, and he was willing to admit that he took chances. There had been a time when he was younger that he hadn't taken as many chances, but the specter of age was creeping up on him, and the compulsion to try and beat the clock became more insistent every day.

Patrick looked at Daisy over his cup and thought about her life. Her shop was at the end of the block, obviously away from the others. He hadn't asked why or if she wanted to move, but she had all of the incentives to strive for more, and still she seemed content with her life.

"Different isn't always bad, so we'll do a once over of the place and see what you have to work with and what you are willing to do," she said as she collected the cups.

"I wanted to thank you for helping me. Friends?" he said as he held out his hand. They shook.

He would have thought with all of the work she did on the land and with plants that her hands might be dry or rough, but they were soft. Soft as her hair looked as it billowed beside her face. She was beautiful. Not in the magazine made up kind of way because as far as he could tell, he had never seen Daisy with a drop of makeup on her. Daisy was beautiful naturally and had inner goodness that seemed to radiate from her. She… Patrick stopped himself. Women had been throwing themselves at him for as long as he could remember. He realized long ago that they didn't know him; they just thought they could smell money on him. He hadn't felt a nibble with any of them, and now, when he finally did feel some attraction to someone, it seemed it was going to be Daisy. He didn't know what shocked him more— that he was attracted to a woman in the midst of this mess or that the woman was the farthest thing from his lifestyle.

Then, as if it were a dream, they both heard the bell of the front door as it opened. Daisy ushered him out the back and waved him on out the door as she handled the incoming customers. Standing outside the store, Patrick looked at the now filled block of cars that had come to buy goods from her.

As he walked towards his car, he realized he just couldn't figure out the people in Sweet Blooms.

"You are a total life saver!" Lisa said as she pushed the portable massage table towards the front door. "My sister, Patience, will be here soon. She called and said she got hung up."

Daisy smiled at her frantic friend. Lisa owned the salon, and they had gotten close once Daisy had made herbal steam for her son to sleep at night. "I'm keeping count so I can collect. Hurry up and attend the bachelorette party."

"Thank you, thank you, thank you." Lisa set the table on its stand and grabbed Daisy into a bear hug. "Having this party come to Sweet Blooms just to be at the salon is such a huge opportunity for me; it's the only reason I'd impose."

"Off with you. I've got a little boy to visit before your sister arrives."

Daisy went over the checklist with her to make sure she had all of her items for the night. "Patience will be here soon enough. I'll set up the munchkin's herbal steam. I'll make sure to take my payment in the form of one of those freshly baked brownies I can smell from here, and no one will be the wiser."

Lisa gave her one more look over her shoulder. "This night couldn't happen without your help."

Daisy put her hand to her head. "Oh, now she says it's true, but will she remember me when she's famous?"

"I'll not only remember you, I'll also name a package after you and charge triple." Lisa tossed that tidbit over her shoulder and loaded up her station wagon to the spa. When Daisy was sure she was on her way, she closed the curtain and turned her attention to the charge inside.

Around lunchtime, Lisa had called. She said her little man wasn't breathing as clearly as he should and wanted to know if Daisy could drop off another sachet for the steam machine. A hint of frustration ran across her brow as she listened to the request. Daisy knew this meant she would have to forgo lunch, go home, gather the herbs, and then bring them back to the shop. Then, after the shop was closed, she'd have to not only deliver them but also make sure they were installed into the steamer correctly and the old sachet was removed. It made no difference; no matter the inconvenience, Daisy knew what her answer would be. After agreeing to come by, Lisa had called again ten minutes after the shop had closed and told Daisy that her sister Patience had been delayed in her arrival. She wanted to know if Daisy could stay after she had installed the sachet until her sister arrived, and, of course, for Daisy, there was only one answer.

Walking into the house, she went to the little prince's room. The room was spacious because he still slept in the modified crib bed. At four years old, he wasn't ready to leave the crib bed for his motor car bed that was against the wall. On the wall, as she walked in the door, was the steam machine quietly sending steam into the air.

Daisy went to get her pack and then set to replacing the sachet. The action was done in minutes. She took the old sachet of wilted herbs and put them into a bag to go back to her home. She'd use the used herbs in her compost, making sure nothing went to waste.

After fixing the machine, she took the time to check on the precious package. She had always had mixed feelings about children. She was an only child. More importantly, she didn't have the family others had. Daisy loved her mother, but she had resolved that children wouldn't be in the mix for her unless she could get the whole package. The whole package to her was two parents, a kid, and a dog.

Lately, she'd begun to think about kids more and more. Who would she leave the store to? Her mother had started training her when she was six years old, and still, Daisy felt as though that hadn't been enough time. Children were becoming a topic that cropped up more and more.

She had met and dated a couple of men in Sweet Blooms, and they were good men, but they weren't men she could imagine as her husband or the father of her children. She knew that staying in Sweet Blooms had severely limited her options. In fact, she had considered leaving and looking abroad, so to speak, via dating sites. Then, when Adam Cade had come, other new people begun to come through, and she had decided to wait.

All of this waiting and so far the only person she seemed attracted to was definitely Mr. Wrong. Daisy shook her head; if it wasn't for bad luck, she thought sometimes she'd have no luck at all. She heard the door close, and it brought her out of her reverie. She exited the baby's room and found Patience in the foyer, with her pajamas on, taking off her coat. She looked up and saw Daisy and sighed.

"Hi Daisy." She hung up her coat and gave Daisy a hug.

"Lisa left for the bachelorette," Daisy said with a smile.

Patience looked up and saw Daisy looking at her clothes. "I know you were wondering why I am in my bunny pajamas. Well, it turns out my loving sister called me an hour ago. I was already in bed. I thought, no problem, I'll just drive over and watch the baby. Little did I know that there would be a random search on the highway because it looks like the police are looking for some men. When I get to the checkpoint, they see me in my pajamas, and they say, 'Ma'am, are you okay?' I tell them, yes, but they start squinting and trying to ask me all sorts of questions until, finally, I got tired and asked what was wrong.

They explained they wanted to do a full search of my car because it looked like I had been taken out of my house against my will. As if that could be the only reason I was running around in my pajamas."

Daisy could see Patience was frustrated. However, on second look, Daisy could see the officer's point of view. Not only did Patience have on her pajamas, but she had rollers in her hair that were covered with a net. Having all of the gear to look beautiful was a gift from Lisa.

Daisy tried to maintain her composure. "I'm sure they meant well."

Patience took another look at Daisy and grinned. "Go ahead and laugh. If you keep it in, you'll turn red and pop."

Daisy laughed and then pointed to the kitchen. "I don't know if it helps, but there are some delicious brownies in the kitchen."

Patience snorted. "It's the least she could have ready for me." As they went into the kitchen, Daisy listened to the trials and tribulations. Patience hadn't meant to seem that way, but Daisy could tell she was starved for attention. She wanted this exchange of the day between her and someone else. She loved working the land and being herself, but the truth was, she was lonely. You could only work the land so much before it became apparent that what was missing from the equation wasn't more work but someone to share it with.

Six

Daisy knew this land. Like she had promised, she had walked over to Patrick's place. It was so funny to say that out loud—Patrick's place. She could see the old second-hand car that Patrick had bought in front of the dilapidated house. Daisy remembered when this house was in tip-top condition not that long ago. She had memories of her mother, Anne, calling Cunningham and being at the house sitting on the now raggedy porch.

She had agreed to come here and look at the land. Now that she was here, she could see the land looked a lot like Patrick. Both of them needed work. The tauntings of Hannah were still rolling around in her head. As she walked closer to the house, little plumes of dust billowed from the dry earth. Still, Daisy was a woman of her word, and she had told Patrick she would come by and give her honest opinion about what could be done with the land.

As if he could hear her thoughts, Patrick stepped out of the front door.

"I've been waiting. I would invite you in, but right now I don't know what I'm more ashamed of, the inside or the outside," he said with a nervous laugh.

For a moment, Daisy stopped in her tracks. This was madness! How could she teach this man to be something he so obviously wasn't. He came down the rickety steps and took them two at a time. As he passed, she could see the little white lines around his mouth.

"Okay, I'm as ready as I'll ever be," he said.

"Okay, let's take a walk, and I'll point out some things, both good and bad."

In an attempt to make sure that it was all business, Daisy thought she may have sounded a little harsh. Patrick didn't seem to mind. He nodded his head and then motioned for her to lead the way. She started to walk, and a cool breeze came by and ruffled her hair. Taking a deep breath, she looked over at Patrick, who gave her a nod to begin.

"The good news is, you have a lot of land. You also have your own water source. If you look behind us, about half a mile up, you'd run into a natural creek, and I know Carl had a couple of wells dug on the property."

"Well, that's good."

Daisy looked at him, and the weight of what he was entrusting her with hit her. If she were a less scrupulous person, she could tell him anything and have him waste his time and money. Stopping, she looked at him with her arms crossed over her chest.

"Patrick, I have to ask you a question."

"Okay."

"Why are you trusting me to lead you in the right direction? You have to know, this is a great opportunity for me to lead you in the wrong direction."

Patrick smiled and ran his hands through his dark hair.

"Daisy, I make a living out of reading people. I knew right away; you were not one of those people to take advantage of a situation. The fact that we are even having this conversation tells me everything I need to know about your character. I haven't known you for a long time, but what I can tell you is that I trust you."

Daisy shook her head and threw her hands up in the air.

"Fine, fine, if that's the way you want to do this, we will do this your way. The truth of it is, you have a lot of land, but none of it has been prepped to do anything with. Replacing the dirt, feeding the soil, we haven't even talked about you picking what you would like to grow. I know the council wants you to do something to show that you are trying to make an effort to really work the land, but I have to tell you, this is going to take a lot of money to get it started."

She didn't know what she expected, but when she looked over at Patrick, she didn't expect to see him smiling.

"How can you be smiling after I just told you all of that bad news?" she asked.

"I'll answer your question, but first I want to ask you a couple of questions. First, are you okay with that?" Patrick said.

"Sure, I'm not the one with a lot of underfed land they need to make into something workable."

"Your land…how long did it take for you to get it that way?"

Daisy stopped. "My mother worked that land, and I continued it after her," she said cautiously.

Patrick must have noticed her reticence and tried to assure her right away.

"I'm not asking to take it. I'm asking so that we can both be on the same page."

"And what page would that be?"

"I want to be able to show the council that the land is being used," he said quickly, keeping her gaze. "Even before you said anything, I thought the same thing that you said."

"I think you will be great once you figure out what you are going to grow."

"I think your words are kind, but I can see you aren't sure if I can do this either. In truth, as reckless as it may appear that I am in other areas, I try not to do something that I don't think I have a good grasp on, and I can tell you I don't have a good grasp on anything that requires growing."

He stopped and looked around the land.

"I have to tell you I wasn't completely honest with you when I told everyone I didn't know my Uncle Carl. I've been here maybe once or twice. I wasn't impressed with it. When I was brought out here, I thought it was a punishment for what happens when I fail. I would get sent into the middle of nowhere."

"If you've thought this all out, why ask me to come out here?"

"I decided I would do what I normally do when I start a new venture. I'd ask a professional. I think I can propose a scenario to help us both."

Daisy waited anxiously. "Who says I need help?"

Patrick eyed her for a moment.

"The shop at the end of the block says you need help. The way I've seen people come out here to see you and how people travel to where you are. The one thing I haven't really seen is you in Sweet Blooms."

Daisy waved him off and tried to shake off the niggling feeling that something he was saying was starting to make sense.

"Patrick, I've been in Sweet Blooms all of my life."

He interrupted. "You've lived here, but it doesn't seem like you've been a part of Sweet Blooms. Now, I can't speak to the why. Maybe they've never noticed. Maybe they think you're happy out here alone, but I told you, Daisy, I make my living reading people. You are not meant to be alone. You are a loving, giving person. You want what the other people in Sweet Blooms have—family and acceptance."

He was wielding his words like daggers, and to Daisy, things that were left unsaid in her heart were laid bare to this man.

"There is an irony to it all that the town wants me to be like them. I have to say to you it's not all it's cracked up to be when a group thinks you're one of them."

Daisy shrugged. "So you say, but then have you ever been somewhere people didn't welcome you?"

Patrick reached out and ran his fingertip along Daisy's jawline. His touch left a trail of tingles that coalesced in her stomach, filling her with anticipation she hadn't known before.

"If we were together, they would have the chance to know you and they'd embrace you."

Daisy flinched and stepped back. "What? Together?" She looked at him incredulously. "I should have known better. Together, he says. I bet. We'll be together, and you'll disappear in the morning—"

"Daisy, stop! I'm not talking about sex!"

She gave him a side eye look. He held up his hands.

"I'm not saying that I wouldn't want… No, what I

mean is you are a very attractive woman, of course, and I'd have to be dead not to notice. This is just getting worse as I go. What I mean is I think we should pretend to be a couple. That way I can say I'm working the land you already have, and you and I can go out into Sweet Blooms, and I can show you the other side."

Daisy heard him, and she could say she believed that he wasn't trying to trick her. She knew he needed to show he was working the land, so the logic held true what he was saying from his point of view. The problem was he had ripped open a scab she thought she had already addressed. She thought about the remarks Hannah had made and realized that while his plan was crazy, it wasn't so crazy that no one would believe it.

All of the other concerns put aside, the issue that bothered her the most was how he had seen when the others hadn't. Her friends who visited her at her home and who came to the shop had never thought to invite her to birthday parties or ask her if she wanted to help out on committees. When it was all said and done, Patrick had seen it and named it. She lived in Sweet Blooms, but she hadn't ever really been a part of Sweet Blooms.

"I know it's out there, so I want to thank you for not saying no right off the bat," he said.

"It's hard to say no to something when it has some merit. I have to say you've been upfront with me, so I'll do you the same."

Patrick smiled. "Here comes that really fair streak."

"I can't give you an answer this second. I need to think about it. I know you don't have a lot of time, and we'd have to do some talking and planning to do this, so I need a day to think it over."

Patrick nodded. "Your answer was better than what I was expecting. I want you to think it over."

Daisy looked at him, at the way he dressed in khakis on a ranch. He had leather loafers in the dust and that determined look on his face, as if he could take on anything. He wasn't like the people of Sweet Blooms, but they had welcomed him and given him a path to become one of them. It hurt. It hurt that this stranger would be able to give her something she should have had from birth.

Her mother had taught her that you didn't sit and mope over things; you made a decision to accept it or change it. Her and Patrick as a couple. That would take a little more talking out in her head.

"Tomorrow then," she said.

"I'll be at the hotel. I don't mind roughing it, but this is a little too close to camping for my taste."

She didn't say anything. She just turned and went towards her house. Did he really say living in the house was like camping? She knew what she wanted, but did she want it at any cost? Daisy didn't know a lot of things, but the thing she was most sure of was tonight was going to be a long night.

Seven

Patrick had told Daisy that he would be in town, but after breakfast, he found himself driving out to the property. He was used to being up early, but getting up early to labor? That was a totally different thing. He had decided that he needed to start with something he knew. He could clean up the inside of the house. How could he expect Daisy to make a decision when he couldn't show her even a sample of him being pseudo competent.

When he arrived, he decided to do low hanging fruit first. He'd take out all of the items that were damaged and put them in front of the house. He'd give the hotel a call and ask them who would pick it up. Come to think of it, how did trash even get picked up on a ranch? He'd work it out.

To get in the spirit of things, Patrick purchased some jeans from the local store, and he pulled out his workout sneakers. He paired the items with a white tee shirt, and he thought he would be cool at the same time he was cleaning. Daisy said she would give him an answer today. He'd at least be able to show her he wouldn't be a complete fish out of water.

About two hours later, Patrick had a new appreciation for those junk removal companies. He was sweaty, his shirt was torn, and he had gone through half of the 24 pack of water. The sad thing was, the only thing he could show for it was moving a table that had been made out of the base of a tree. He looked at the other pieces of furniture, and now they all looked great.

He decided to go into town for lunch and a broom and mop. At this point, he wasn't sure he could even lift a fork to his mouth, but he was determined to not have Daisy find him face down in the place before they could even begin the deal. He could acknowledge it was pride, and he gathered himself to leave the house.

As he sat in the car and his hands trembled from the work, he had to admit that he felt accomplished. It had been a long time since he had done anything with his own two hands.

"I have to say, all of the secrecy is intriguing," Hannah said as Daisy walked into her home. She smiled at Daisy and wiggled her eyebrows. "Just like you asked, I made sure there was no one here today but you and me. I've got no one staying in the house and Nathan is with his father today. So for all intents and purposes, the coast is clear."

Daisy was the closest to Hannah in the whole town. Both of them shared a similar background and had more than once talked about the lack of being accepted in Sweet Blooms. Hannah was a beautiful woman who had found her true love with Adam Cade. Being with Hannah gave her hope that true love could happen for her as well.

"I need a very open minded friend to talk to."

Hannah's smile faded, and she showed Daisy to the couch and settled in.

"I'm more than open minded; I'm on your side," Hannah said slowly. "I've never seen you like this, so serious."

"It is serious." Daisy took a deep breath and looked her in the eye. "I need to talk through an improbable situation, and I need someone who can listen and tell me if I've gone too far as well."

Hannah nodded. "I've got you. Go for it."

The moment was here for Daisy to say something, but the words wouldn't come. What made it worse was the way Hannah was so eager to help her. The unconditional help Hannah was offering without even knowing what the problem said volumes to Daisy.

Hannah reached out and placed her hand on top of Daisy's.

"What's going on, Daisy?"

The touch was almost enough to push Daisy over the edge and send her into a crying fit of gratefulness.

Taking a deep breath, she blurted it out. "It's about not being a true member of Sweet Blooms."

Hannah knew about Daisy's feeling of being needed in Sweet Blooms but not being a part of it. She knew that after the death of her mother, there was a hole in her life where she wanted to put a family. Daisy didn't want to settle for someone to make it better; she wanted the right person. Until Hannah met Adam, she had doubted if there was such a thing as the right person for anyone.

"Go on."

"It's getting worse, this emptiness that I have," Daisy

told her. "I need to start looking if I want to find someone."

Hannah patted her hand. "I told you going out would be good for you, but only if you're ready. And remember, never because you feel desperate."

"Well, a unique situation has appeared that may help me with that."

"Okay, what situation?"

Daisy looked at Hannah square in the eyes. "Patrick offered me a deal. He would be my boyfriend, love interest, and I would let him use my plot of land as proof that we were working the land. I thought this would be a good way for me to learn how to even date or act around men, and a way for me to see the men in Sweet Blooms and for Sweet Blooms to see me differently."

Hannah sat back on the sofa and just looked at Daisy.

"You and Patrick?"

"Y-yes."

"The city guy who couldn't tell one end of a hammer from the other if we gave him directions?"

Daisy nodded. "I spoke with him, and we are both in a situation where maybe we can help each other. He needs to give proof to the board. The board wouldn't really believe it unless we say we were in a relationship, and I would get the practice."

"Well, what I can say is I didn't see that coming." Hannah cleared her throat and sat back up. "Well, no one is going to fault you on taste," she said with a smile.

"You know looks don't matter to me. I want to say there is more to him than I thought. After talking to him, I realize he's not as shallow as I thought he would be." Daisy let out the breath she had been holding now that she had finally said it out loud. "The problem is, I don't know if I'm being stupid. That is why we are doing the cloak and dagger routine today. That's why I wanted to make sure we were all alone, so just in case I am being dumb, you could call me an idiot in private."

Hannah laughed. "If you looked up the word caution, we'd find your picture. There are a lot of things that might come up with your name, but idiot isn't one of them. I can definitely say when I suggested you get out more, this wasn't what I had in mind, but I'm your friend, and I'm used to you thinking outside of the box.

"We joke about it, but you know it's not about Sweet Blooms, right?"

Daisy nodded. "It's me. I should be happy with me regardless of what others may or may not think. Most days, I am. But there are days when I'm hanging the herbs or doing something else, and I say, 'what's wrong with me that I'm all alone?'"

Hannah gave her a hug and smiled at her. "First off, there is nothing wrong with you at all. Second, addressing the problem of practice is a good thing with Patrick as long as you are both aware of the rules of what is going on."

Daisy nodded.

Hannah smiled. "Let me say these words to you as someone who thought they knew what was going on as well when love ran up and grabbed my attention."

"Love?"

"Yes, the four letter word we never talk about. Patrick is attractive and now listening to you. He's a nice guy and—"

Daisy waved her hands. "No, no, no, it's not like that. We may be friends by the end of this, that I'll give you, but this is more business than anything else. We know the rules, and we plan on keeping them. He has a life to go back to, and I have a life I want to start."

"Well, if all of that is a go, what are you waiting for?"

"We're waiting for me. If I tell him yes, what is it that I should expect? I'm practicing, but what if he's no good at it?"

Hannah laughed. "First of all, I think a man who looks like Patrick has had a decent amount of practice of how to be around women. There are no rules, Daisy, when it comes to relationships. This isn't a plant that has a regimen or prescribed way for things to be done. I have no books to give you to research."

Daisy knew she looked skeptical, and Hannah pushed on.

"You'll discover what you like and don't like. It's about finding you and doing what you like."

"I thought you were going to be a lot more helpful."

Hannah tsked. "You thought I was going to give you some rules and safety guidelines for you to hide in, but I have none, my love. This is something you are going to have to trust yourself to lead the way and determine what is right for you.

Although the idea sounded different when you said it at first, I have to say now it's starting to grow on me. I think this was a gift in disguise."

Daisy stayed and talked about the upcoming wedding, and the specialist Hannah had finally found to do the wedding. They talked about venues and food. When she left, Daisy felt better about her decision. She just needed to tell Patrick.

Daisy thought she was a patient person. She grew plants that only flowered biannually; certainly, she could wait until the end of the day to let Patrick know about her decision. It was a busy day at the shop because the end of the school year was coming, and there were several parties, corsages, and floral decorations being requested during this time of year. Even with all of the arrangements she made, Daisy knew her attention wasn't on her work today.

She had finished the afternoon rush when she realized it had taken a little more out of her than she had expected. After making sure that all of the arrangements that were due today were sent out, she closed up her shop and went home. When she arrived in front of her house, she shouldn't have been surprised, but she was, to see Patrick standing there.

He was dressed in jeans and had a water bottle sitting on her bench with a box in his hand. The jeans were so crisp she knew he hadn't had them for long. The shirt was white with short sleeves. She was mildly irritated because she knew she was sweaty from the day's work, and he looked fresh and calm sitting on her bench.

"Am I on a clock?" Daisy snapped at him. She instantly felt bad because she knew he wasn't the problem; she was just anxious. Snapping at the person who you wanted to have a relationship with was probably not the way to start out.

He didn't even bother to give her his full attention. "I take it you're not into friendly reminders."

"Friendly reminder? How can it be a reminder if I'm the one who said I would get back to you. Maybe I see you as a little pushy."

Patrick shook his head. "I'm just trying to make myself available to you."

Daisy walked over to the bench and sat down. "I don't know what your favorite color is or if you even have one."

"It's blue."

Daisy waited. "Well?"

Patrick laughed. "Your favorite color is green."

She looked at him, waiting for the rest of it.

"You think this because?"

"Because every time I see you, you have something green on."

"Don't you think it's kinda creepy to be looking at someone that closely all the time?"

He sat up and looked at her finally.

"I'll tell you, I don't look at people all the time. From the very beginning, I've noticed you, and after we spoke, I was more intrigued. So if the question was do I gawk at beautiful women and stare at them, the answer would be no."

Daisy got up and began to pace in front of the bench.

"I take it you've decided." His voice was clear and level as if this wasn't the huge decision it was. She could feel heat radiating from his body. Did he make these kinds of offers casually? Why wasn't he as wound up as she was?

"How was your day?" he asked. The question stopped her in her tracks.

"What did you ask me?"

"Your day. How was your day?"

"I went to work," she said incredulously as if she were confused by the obvious answer.

"I brought you something," he said as he gave her the box.

"What for?"

"I bought you a gift because sometimes couples give each other gifts."

"Couples?"

"I assumed from your behavior you've decided to help me but aren't sure how it works."

"And you know how this works?"

"Not exactly, but I have an idea of what's going to happen."

"Good, or at least I think that's good. Do you go around doing this kind of thing often?"

Patrick grinned at her. "I think you are asking me if I am a boyfriend for hire."

"No, of course not. I mean, you're not, are you? Never mind, forget the question. I've decided yes to do this."

"Why? I know why I asked you to do it, but I want to know why you agreed," he asked.

Daisy took a moment, looked at the box in her hand and the man on her bench, and said what came to mind.

"You told the good and bad. You told me the truth about your and my situation. After talking to you, I like you as a person. I trust you." She thought the words would make him feel better or at least smile, but instead, after she said it, he lost his smile and stood up.

"I'm going to help you, Daisy, because you are a good person. I've had all day to think about it, and you accepting just proves how nice a person you are. We can be friends, and I think that's great, but don't trust me, Daisy."

"What sense does that make?"

"I'm here for a moment, and the one thing meeting you has shown me is that I am not one of the good people. We can be friends, but don't trust me."

<h1 style="text-align:center">Eight</h1>

"Don't you think telling me not to trust you is a problem? And why not?"

Before Patrick could answer the question, they heard a car arriving. When it pulled up, it kicked up so much dust that both of them had to turn away. It was a red sport Ferrari. Ferraris weren't seen in Sweet Blooms everyday, if ever, so Patrick had a sinking feeling he knew who it was.

All of the reasons that he had kept from Daisy about why he couldn't be trusted had just driven up in front of her house. Before the blonde tipped hair could be seen, Patrick knew.

His body tensed, and his blood pumped twice as fast through his veins. It was like that moment before you found out who the mole was on those reality television shows. The slam of the door confirmed his arrival. Damien Tyler stood against the side of the car, smiling at him as if he had never left the city.

"Patty!"

Patrick plastered a smile on his face and walked towards Damien. He was taking in his surroundings as he was walking towards him. Patrick knew that by the time their hands had met, Damien would have a total resell value for everything from the bench in Daisy's yard to her house. Damien was about five foot eight, not so tall. He wore a tailored suit and his hair was cut low on the sides and about two inches on top. The top of his hair was still frosted with blonde highlights.

Damien was close to fifty but looked like he was still in his forties. Damien was his partner in crime, his wingman, and in the past had been one of the few he could call to get him out of jams.

"Patty, you don't look so glad to see me. I mean, I even got you some decent wheels in this backward hole. I don't get a thank you at least?"

Patrick gripped his hand and welcomed him. He didn't say anything because he could feel Daisy's eyes boring into his back.

"What are you doing out here and where did you get that car?" he asked.

"I came to see what was taking you so long, and I used the letter from the will as collateral to get the car. I figured when you finished selling the land, you'd have more than enough funds."

"Damien, I wish you wouldn't have done that. I don't know that you can use the land as collateral. Things are a little different here in Sweet Blooms."

Damien peered around Patrick.

"Maybe the reason you aren't so welcoming has to do with the little lady behind you?"

Patrick didn't like the way Damien sounded, and he had no intention of introducing him to Daisy if he could avoid it.

"She's got nothing to do with anything. Let's go to my place; it's up the road," Patrick said, pointing behind Damien. For a moment, Patrick wasn't sure what Damien would do. Then, at the last moment, Damien saluted to Daisy before calling out, "Maybe some other time, little lady." He gave an exaggerated bow and then got back into the car. Patrick waved to what appeared to be a very confused Daisy. He couldn't explain now, but he hoped Damien showing up hadn't ruined their agreement.

The ride was so short they didn't even speak. When they pulled up in front of the house, Damien whistled.

Damien got out of the car and took in the surroundings. Patrick knew what he saw. If he was honest, he probably saw what he had first seen—a dilapidated home that would be worth more demolished.

"Why are you still here, Patty?" Damien asked.

Patrick glanced around his place and thought about him and Daisy. "I'm working on it. Sweet Blooms isn't like everything else. They have their own way. I can't just sell the land, so I have to meet the conditions of the local board."

Damien's eyes crinkled with laughter. "What are you saying, that you can't move some small time board? Are they making you jump through hoops?"

Patrick smiled. "I guess you could say so, but it's not a problem. I've got it under control."

Damien snorted. "If you hanging out with the blonde is your way of managing things, no wonder it's taking you so long to leave here."

Patrick shook his head. "She's helping me out, Damien. I know you are trying to help me, but I need to follow these rules, and I'll be here for the next two months."

"Two months?"

"I told you it's complicated. I have to deal with the local board, and then I have to make sure I meet their conditions. Anyway, the long and short of it is I'll be here for two months."

Patrick stood his ground and waited. He and Damien had been through these conversations so many times that he had lost count. When money was involved, Damien would always ask for it faster, quicker, and larger. Patrick believed in relying on steady results to get his gains. In the past, these conversations had never really bothered Patrick, but today was different. He didn't want to look too closely at what made this different. Patrick wasn't sure if the difference was the place or a very special woman.

Throwing his hands up in the air, Damien gave in.

"If you are committed to doing this their way, so be it," he said in mock surrender. Patrick wasn't fooled by his gracious capitulation. He could already see Damien angling for the next move. Why did Damien's moves look so circumspect now? They had been together for a long time looking for the big hit, but today… Patrick shook it off. He wouldn't think about it.

"Damien, you came a long way out here to find me. You must have had a reason."

Damien smiled and went back to the car, running his hands over the hood.

"I came here because it seemed like you were taking a bit of time. I mean, the money from this land is going to set us up big. You know we've been making money together for a while."

Patrick looked at Damien and saw the grey hair at his temples and the rings on his fingers and that ever-present smile.

"We're not married, Damien; we're business partners at best. Listen, Damien, I'm not saying we don't do well together. What I'm saying is let's not make it personal."

Damien smiled. "When isn't it personal when money is involved?"

"What are you saying?"

"I'm saying I'm getting up there in years. That last investment, I was going to take my part and settle down. I'm looking to get that back and then settle for a bit."

"And?" Patrick prompted, waiting for the punch line.

The smile fell away from Damien's face, and he came around the car to stand in front of Patrick.

"Well, if you want it straight."

"I do."

"I invested in the last deal because of you. I lost the money for me to settle down. I think you owe me that money back."

"Owe you? It was a chance you took."

"On your say so! I'm an old man, and I need my money. So do whatever you need to do here and give me my cash." Damien backed away and went to get into the car. "Let what I said sink in. I don't think it'll do for me to keep talking to you today. I've got a place at the hotel so you can reach me there."

"Tight but not so tight you can't afford a hotel room?"

"It's a small town. There weren't many options. I'll be in touch, and you do what you need to do to get my money," Damien said as he pulled out of the driveway and made his way down the hill. Damien was already out of earshot when Patrick replied, "Yeah, it's nice to see you too."

Patrick turned and looked towards Daisy's place. He didn't know what to tell her. He felt foolish. He had come to Sweet Blooms and gotten caught up in the innocence of the town. He was here to get the money and leave. He just had to remember that.

Nine

"I think the first rule that couples have is that they talk about everything," Daisy said as she wrapped roses in paper.

Daisy had been waiting for Patrick. She wasn't sure how he was going to approach her, but after not meeting his friend, she knew it was on Patrick to come to her. She had stayed up late last night thinking he would come, but when no one showed up at midnight, she knew he wasn't coming. This morning she was glad he showed up but was a little cross at him for taking so long.

"He's a person I've done business with in the city. He came out here to help me with the selling of the land."

"Is that all?" she asked.

Patrick looked at her and sighed. "That's as much as I can say and still tell you the truth."

"I asked for the truth, and you gave it. Since I was way off in thinking you were coming in to talk about your guest, why did you come by this morning?"

"I realized we didn't go over ground rules. I have some questions I need to ask you, and you can ask me as well."

Daisy was suspicious already, but she nodded.

"Are you currently dating anyone?" he asked.

"No, and you?"

Patrick laughed. "I'm not, but if I were, there would be no way she would still be with me as long as I've been in Sweet Blooms." When his laughs subsided, he walked up to the counter and leaned on it until he was inches away from her shoulder.

"You do realize we are going to have to be close to one another."

She was frozen in place. The only thing she could do was nod her head.

"Generally speaking, couples tend to be close, and I wanted to make sure you were okay with that."

"Yes," she replied. Was that even her voice? It was more of a raspy yes than the firm adult yes she wanted to portray.

"Also, we are going to be going out and being seen in town. Do you have any dietary restrictions?"

"Dietary restrictions?"

Patrick smiled. "Yes, it will look very odd if I take the woman I'm with to a steak house, but everyone knows she's a vegetarian. That's going to blow the cover."

"Blow the cover, yes." She knew she sounded like a simpleton. He was worried about making the plan work. She had to mentally shake herself; this wasn't real.

"No, I'm not a vegan. I can eat everything, and I have no allergies."

"Good, let's get started." Daisy heard the words come out of his mouth, and then he held out his hand. She looked at it and them him.

"Put your hand in mine, Daisy. I mean, certainly, we can hold hands."

It was such a simple request, but when she looked at his hand, it seemed like so much more. She picked up a towel next to the roses and dried off her hand. She was stalling, and she didn't know why. Finally, she lifted her hand and placed it in his.

His hands were warm and firm. She didn't know what she expected. Maybe she thought all city guys had soft hands. These hands had a callus or two on them. These were hands that did work. They were good gardening hands.

"Thank you, Daisy."

She looked up and there he was. Those eyes that seemed to suck her in and that voice that radiated comfort like a warm day. He left and promised to be back when she closed up shop. She tried to tell him that he didn't have to come back, but he insisted this was a couple thing to do.

Anticipation had her floating on clouds wondering what they would do tonight. All of that came crashing to a halt when Patrick's friend came in the door. Daisy saw him walk in through the door and take inventory of her entire shop before making his way to the counter. She knew this man was more than Patrick had let on, and curiosity was beating at her door to find out exactly what their connection was.

"Can I help you?" Daisy asked as he approached the counter.

"No, not really, I just came in to see the flowers and to see if Patty was here."

The words that came out of his mouth were cool and welcoming, but his eyes were dark and fathomless.

"Sorry, Patrick isn't here."

"Ah, well, perhaps it's for the best. Is it possible that I could have a word with you?"

"I'm afraid you have me at a disadvantage. It seems like you know who I am, but I don't know who you are."

"Excuse my manners. My name is Damien Tyler, and I'm an investment broker. I find deals that will potentially make people money and then invest their money for them."

"I'm Daisy, the owner of this shop, and I'm not sure what we would have to talk about."

"Young lady, I'm here to talk to you about Patty, of course."

Daisy heard the bell ring, signaling someone else had come into the shop. She didn't even look up from Damien. He reminded her of a garden snake. His smile only made it worse.

"Today isn't a good day for me. Maybe we can plan to meet in town sometime this week, and I can make sure Patrick is there as well?"

"Our conversation shouldn't take long. Patty and I are old friends. I just want to understand what the hold up is regarding the land. You know he's a business partner as well, so I just want to make sure everything is moving along and there aren't any hindrances."

Daisy straightened her back and looked him in the eye.

"Hindrances? I'm not clear on what you're looking for or what you'd like to discuss, but again, at my workplace is not the time or place. Since this is involving Patrick's land, I wouldn't discuss anything without having him at the table. Now, my advice to you is to talk to Patrick. If you two are as close as you believe, then you should have no problems discussing the specifics."

For a moment, she saw Damien lose his nice demeanor. He recovered it so quickly she almost missed it.

"Ms.—?"

"Hello, Daisy, can you wrap me up a bouquet of something special and have it sent to the courthouse? The board will be having a meeting today, and I'd like there to be fresh flowers on the table," Clarissa said as she interrupted what Damien was about to say.

Daisy had never been so happy to see Clarissa in her life. She smiled at Clarissa, and then she nodded.

"I'll have to get some flowers that just came in from the back," Daisy said.

Clarissa waved her on. "Go ahead. Don't worry, I'll keep your guest occupied."

Daisy didn't question it. She was so relieved that Clarissa was here to interfere that she was about to make a bouquet that showed her gratitude.

The curvy brunette next to him was attractive, but Damien wasn't here for her. He needed to understand what was going on between the blonde and Patty. Before Damien had come to the town, he had already done his research to get an idea of the value of the land. When he had finished drawing up the papers with the potential of upselling because it was the home of the owner of Cade Designs, he was able to get a line of credit that had gotten him the car and a nice condo. Of course, he had to draw up papers saying him and Patty were in business, and he was acting on Patty's behalf, but he knew when Patty was back home, he would understand and forgive him.

"Well, Daisy will be occupied for a minute or two. I heard you asking about Patrick Cunningham and the board," Clarissa said.

Damien looked at the brunette again. If he could take care of two birds with one stone, so be it.

"Yes, I'm told he had to see them to sell the land," he prompted, turning towards her to give her his full attention.

"Yes, he did. I know because I'm a board member."

Damien looked at the woman and thought his luck hadn't run out on him as he had feared. "You? You look too pretty to be on the board."

Clarissa batted her eyelashes and gave him a coy smile. "Mr. Tyler, perhaps we could help one another. Would you like to take a walk?"

Damien thought about the heat outside and started to say no, but when he looked at Clarissa and her high heels, he figured she wouldn't be able to make it far, or better yet, when he showed her his car, she just might want to take a drive in it.

"I'd be delighted to take a walk with you."

"Daisy, I'm taking Mr. Tyler off of your hands."

Damien followed her out of the floral shop. When he pointed to his car, she smiled and said, "I hope it's a rental and not a buy."

Damien nodded but said nothing as he seethed walking next to her. He asked about the board, but she diverted the question and said that the walk was invigorating and should be enjoyed. Twelve blocks later, Damien was sure he had a line of sweat running down his shirt. Clarissa, on the other hand, still looked refreshed. In fact, the only hint that they had walked was a slight flush to her cheeks. Finally, she stopped at a coffee shop. When she sat down, a waitress came over, and she ordered for them both.

"Two glasses of water and two caramel macchiatos."

"I don't think—" Damien started but didn't get a chance to speak because the waitress left right away to fulfill Clarissa's wish. Once the waitress was gone, Damien opened his mouth to speak, but Clarissa leaned across the table and put her finger over his lips.

"We are not here to have a conversation the way you'd like to have it. I'm here to explain some things to you because you're new. Do you understand?"

Damien sat back as he tried to catch his breath. When Clarissa's finger left his lips, he knew he was in trouble.

"Mr. Tyler, this is Sweet Blooms. We are a small town with small town values. Every member has their part to play. I understand that you are from the city and this relationship doesn't seem natural to you, so I'm going to help you."

Just then, the waitress came and delivered the glasses of water. Damien was ready to tell Clarissa she had it all wrong. He didn't know what he had done to offend her, but he wanted to make it up to her. Really, Damien was thinking that if she wasn't on the board, he wouldn't have taken the walk.

"Clarissa, I think we've gotten on the wrong foot and—"

"No, I don't believe we did. You see, this morning I walked into Daisy's shop to pick up some flowers to lift my spirits and I saw you in there trying to pump her for information. We're a small town, and we have plenty of dysfunctional habits, but the one thing we do know how to do is to protect our own. So hear me and please understand that I'm serious. If you have business with Patrick Cunningham, please make sure to find him and ask him,"

"I didn't think—"

"That is probably the first honest thing I've heard come out of your mouth."

The waitress came by and delivered the two macchiatos.

"The drinks are for you on your way back. We live in a small town, Mr. Tyler, it doesn't mean we are a part of the land time forgot. If I find you harassing Daisy again, I'll call a meeting and tell everyone on the board that we need to keep the land in the town's possession indefinitely.

I want to thank you for this talk and your time."

Damien watched Clarissa walk away from the table, leaving him with a warning and a long walk back to his car. Sweet Blooms wasn't the easy mark he thought it would be, but with so much money on the line, he wasn't about to walk away from Sweet Blooms and his best friend, Patty.

Ten

The front bell rung, and Daisy sighed in exhaustion. It was closing time. She was cleaning up, and the prospect of having to deal with one more customer wasn't on her top list of things to do. She looked up at the clock and saw it was ten to four. She could always say she was closed, but her sign said four, and she'd stay until four.

"I'm coming out. Give me a minute."

"It's no problem. I've got a minute to spare," replied the deep male voice.

Daisy smiled at Patrick's reply. When she reached the front of the store, she saw Patrick standing in the middle of the store. Did he practice his best poses, or was it natural that every pose he struck made it seem like he was ready for a photo shoot?

What was she supposed to say to him now? They had made an agreement; she had no problem with her part about teaching him about the land, but this couple thing...

Before when he came around, she was suspicious, and now when he came around, her stomach was tied in knots.

He had said earlier that they would be close. He'd already held her hand; how much closer did they really have to be? She was standing behind the counter like it was a defense barrier. This agreement made everything so complicated all of a sudden.

"I'd pay money to hear all of the machinations going on in your head," Patrick said, interrupting her thoughts.

"I'm sorry?"

Patrick walked to the counter and leaned over it until he was once again eye level to her.

"I said that you are thinking so much and so hard that I can see the smoke rising from your head."

"Now look who's imagining things."

"I think I know the problem, and I'm here with a solution."

"First, I didn't say I agreed there was a problem, but let's hear it."

"It has occurred to me that you are a woman who likes schedules. Your plants grow on schedule. You keep the schedule of hours for the shop religiously. I can tell because you should have called out to me to say you were closed, but you didn't. Yes, I think this whole couple thing will be less stressful for you if we put it on a schedule, so you'll know what's happening."

Daisy heard him, but she wasn't sure that what he was proposing was going to help. It was like telling everyone the girl was going to be eaten by the monster in the next frame. Did that make anyone feel better?

"Okay, Mr. Problem Solver, you've given this some thought if you've come up with a schedule, so how long will this take?"

"For as long as you're helping me with the land. I think that's fair."

Daisy looked at him, wide-eyed. "Really? What can take that long with couples? I see them all the time in Sweet Blooms, and none of them look that busy."

Patrick laughed. "I'm not sure if you just complimented or insulted the relationships in Sweet Blooms. This is going to require more explanation than I thought, but it's okay; I'm up to the task. So why don't we try this? Tomorrow we will start the day as a couple. I'll come by in the morning."

"It's your call. I think we should start with dinner."

Patrick grinned. "I think you're stalling."

Daisy smiled. "No problem. I'll give over to your better judgment."

"Good. With that settled, I need to be on my way to make sure I'm prepared."

Daisy shook her head. "Personally, I think you need your rest, but what do I know? You're the expert on couples."

Patrick stood up and gave her an exaggerated bow.

"You are right. I'm the expert, and I'll see you in the morning."

Daisy watched as Patrick left and shook her head. She started to think about the women she saw in Sweet Blooms. Every now and again she thought she heard sighs of indulgence, but there were no children around. Daisy didn't think Patrick really understood what it was to be a couple with her, and if all men in Sweet Blooms were as stubborn as Patrick, it would explain the indulgent smiles she occasionally saw.

Daisy looked at Patrick sleeping on the oversized couch. He was a handsome man to look at even in sleep. He wore a light blue tee shirt and matching plaid sleep pants. Who went to bed color coded?

She had knocked on the door, and when he didn't answer, she used the old key with the hopes that it would work and it did. The sun had just set, and it was time to tend the land. She could admire him later; now it was time to wake. She tapped on his shoulder, but he just moaned.

"Patrick? Patrick, it's time to wake up."

"It can't be," he said and rolled over on the couch.

Daisy shook his shoulder. "I asked you about this yesterday. You wanted to talk about couples this morning, but we've got land to attend to."

Patrick turned to face her with one eye open. "Is the land moving or going somewhere that we can't address it when the sun comes up?"

Daisy snorted. "The land will be fine, but if you try to water land after the sun comes up and you don't start beforehand, the water bill will quadruple. So if you want to wait, I'll go back to my place, and you let me know when you're ready."

"Quadruple?"

"It happens like that when you are trying to water before the sun evaporates it."

Patrick groaned and rolled onto the floor. "It doesn't look like it, but I'll be ready in ten minutes."

Daisy smiled.

"No problem. I'll wait outside." She looked over her shoulder to see Patrick crawling to the bathroom, and it took all of her willpower not to laugh. However, true to his word, he was out ten minutes later, looking as if he had been awake all morning.

"Please tell me you have coffee at your place?"

"I do, but I don't usually have any until I set up the watering."

Patrick grumbled and shook his head. Daisy swore she heard him say something about how coffee deprivation was inhumane.

After a twenty-minute walk towards her house, Patrick broke the silence.

"Where do you keep the watering hoses?"

She smiled. "The hoses are underground. I don't have a large patch of land to water, so I have a long string of ten twenty-foot hoses lining the lanes of my patch. Then I put holes all along with the hose, so when I turn on the water, it will water everything. The problem is that it takes a while for the water to make it all the way, so I have to turn on the water early when the pressure is high to make it along the way."

They walked to a small machine that came up about knee high. Patrick looked at the tank and then back at Daisy.

"Where do you fill the tank from?"

"From below. This tank and machine sit on top of a well. That's why the patch is here a little too far from my house or yours. The well decided where I would plant."

Patrick looked at the distance between the two houses.

"What happens in the winter?"

"Thank goodness we don't have harsh winters. The weather drops maybe from 80 to 60. During those times, I have to put up a structure and cover it with plastic to create a mini greenhouse, so my herbs don't die."

"You do this by yourself?"

"No, I hire a group of kids from the high school to help me out."

Daisy could feel him staring at her.

"What?"

"You always find new ways to surprise me."

Daisy snorted. "You're not that hard to surprise, then. Come on, I'll get your coffee so you can think."

As Patrick looked into the dark depths of the coffee cup and let the smell flood his senses, he knew Daisy was right. He needed coffee to think. He looked at her across the table and saw her smiling behind a cup that read Bless These Hands.

"Now that you're here, I think we should talk about the couple thing."

"Okay."

He saw her place her cup down and sit up straighter. He could see she was bracing herself to deliver what she thought was going to be big news. He'd been waiting for some type of push back; he just wasn't sure what her rationale was going to be to back out.

"I don't think we should do the couple thing. Maybe we can do a consultant thing," she told him.

"You mean you can water the herbs by yourself?"

She blew out a breath and looked at him as if he were still asleep. "No, I'm not talking about the water thing. I'm talking about us being a couple in Sweet Blooms thing."

He put his cup down and then leaned back in the chair. "Couples talk to each other all the time. Would you like to tell me why you are having second thoughts?"

"Well, look at your friend Damien. He's from a different kind of living, and that means you are too."

He looked at his coffee cup as he tried to decipher exactly what she was saying. "So is your thought that couples in the city are different than couples in small towns and I may not be qualified?"

She rolled her eyes and tapped her fingers on the table. "I'm saying that if I wanted to do the couple thing, maybe I should do it with someone who's had the same experiences as I've had. What are we going to talk about in town? No one will believe we have any common ground at all."

He smiled. She was worried about if they were compatible? "So what I'm hearing is you don't think I know enough of your interests as a woman?"

She gasped. "What?"

He reached out and placed his hand atop hers on the kitchen table. "Do you need me to say the question in a different way, maybe? You don't think a guy like me can be with a woman like you because I'm not a local?"

She looked at his hand atop hers, and then she faced him. "If that's the way you want to say it."

"Couples are all over the world, and it's not about where you come from, it's all about the chemistry between the couple."

"Well, there's no chemistry between us."

"Do you find me unattractive, Daisy?"

"That's not a fair question."

"Really?"

"I have to say yes, no matter what. If I do, then I have to say yes, and if I don't, polite manners demand that I tell you that you are attractive if not my type. Which is what I've been trying to say to you. We're too different."

Patrick kept lightly stroking her hand on the table. He could feel the slight tremble beneath his fingertips.

"Chemistry is the beginning, Daisy. It won't hold a relationship, but it can ignite a spark. When a couple finds common ground, then they fan the spark."

"We have no common ground!"

"I think we just watered it this morning."

She swallowed and then looked into his eyes. "I'm already odd. I'm scared, and I don't want anyone to laugh at me."

"Laugh at you?"

"The only reason you're with me is because of the land, Patrick."

He looked at her and then stood up, taking her hand with him. He remembered he saw what he was looking for on the back of the entrance door. When Daisy stood up, he walked them out of the kitchen and to the front door. When they were standing in front of the mirror, he stopped.

"What do you see?"

He could see her eyes darting between them in the reflection. Her hands were at her sides fidgeting when she shrugged her shoulders. "This is silly."

He shook his head and nodded toward the mirror.

"I see a complex woman who, on the outside, is one of the most beautiful women I've ever met. Blonde hair that shimmers, brown oval eyes that are brimming with knowledge, and skin that women pray for. A person has only to really look at you to know the reason why every man is going to take a second look at you, and you haven't even spoken yet. No, Daisy, no one with eyes will be laughing at you. They'll all be wondering how I managed to get you to be with me."

She stared at him as if she were trying to divine if he was telling the truth.

"I don't see what you see, but I'll go along with this. When do we do the couple things?"

"I'll give you a heads up the day before. I want to make sure we get all of our work done as well, and I know you have the flower shop."

She smiled at him in the mirror. "So it's a standing date where we'll water the land?"

"We're a couple; we can take turns watering the land."

Daisy laughed. "Okay, when do you water?"

"You'll water the first week, and I'll do the next."

"Okay, Mr. Farmer."

Patrick shook his head and told her he would meet with her later. He had to go buy watering clothes. When she heard that, she did laugh out loud as he went out the door.

Eleven

Hannah had pointed out that when Daisy was doing a wedding or event outside of the store, she had to close the shop because she had no help. Hannah had suggested she advertise for an assistant. When Daisy heard the idea, she thought no one would apply, but she was wrong. She had received a large response, and now she was down to two promising candidates.

She was having such a dilemma in choosing that she called Hannah over to the shop. It didn't help that Patrick had sent her a text saying they would have dinner at his place tonight. At his place. She didn't recall a dining table in the place when she went yesterday morning. Daisy shook her head to try and clear away the anticipation of what Patrick would do for dinner tonight.

When the bell rang, a sigh of relief went through Daisy as she walked to the front of the store. In blue jeans, a white top, and her hair in a messy ponytail, Hannah came into the store all smiles.

"How are the wedding plans going?" Daisy asked.

Hannah's smile dimmed. "I fired another planner. I'm hoping this other planner on the list will be a better fit."

"What's the problem?"

"All of the planners seem to have their own vision on what the wedding should be because Cade has money. The first argument is always the dress."

"The dress? That's your choice last time I heard."

"Well, the kicker is I want a blue dress," Hannah said and crossed her hands over her chest as if she were waiting for a fight.

Daisy just said, "Oh."

"You are taking this better than any of the wedding planners," Hannah said.

Daisy could see Hannah getting fidgety. She held out her hands and smiled.

"Today we tackle my problems and tomorrow we tackle yours, deal?"

Hannah nodded. "So what problems do you have today?"

Daisy walked to the back and showed her the two applications she had.

"Hannah, this is all your doing. I have these two applications left. One of them is a college person—a young woman named Tate—and the other is John's aunt, you know the one who is a twin. I like them both."

"Well, there are a couple of things to consider. Not that I'm an authority, but being with Adam and running the B&B, I would ask some questions like who has the most experience and does either one have an advantage in doing the task? Do you know what the tasks are?"

Daisy nodded. "I'll need someone to open and close the shop. They need to be able to take orders for the day, and I'll show them some basic arrangements, so they need to be able to multi-task. They also need to be able to use the computers and phone."

Hannah gave her the thumbs up. "Good, your tasks are defined. Tell me why you chose these two."

"I chose Tate because she's young, understands the technology, and has a good personality. I chose John's aunt because she's patient. She has prior knowledge of flowers, but the problem there is she admitted she's not good with computers. Time is short, so I may not be able to give her all the time she needs to run things."

"I think you've outlined both candidates well and you have a good idea of what will be required. When all else fails, consider this: who would you rather be in the store with all day long?"

"John's aunt."

Hannah smiled. "Who do you feel would be able to hit the ground running and watch the store if you had to go to a wedding next week?"

"Tate."

"In this case, since they both satisfy a need you have, I would tell you to call upon your women's intuition and go with that."

"My gut says John's aunt, but my business sense says Tate."

"Well, there's good news and bad news. The good news is both candidates live in Sweet Blooms so you can find them and offer them trials. The bad news you won't know who is really suited until they are tested on the job."

"Hannah, I was hoping for a little more help."

"I know you hate making mistakes, but right now, your guess is as good as mine."

Hannah stayed for another twenty minutes, and then she was out and off to find out if the other wedding planner had answered back.

Daisy walked to the back of the store and looked at the event calendar she had open on the small table. She was going to be booked for the next month. She needed to make a decision. She thought about what Hannah said, and then she went ahead and listened to her business sense. She wanted someone who would hit the ground running. She looked in her phone contacts and found Tate's number.

Damien was hitting a wall. Patty wouldn't return his calls. The few times he had waited for him at the house, Patty had told him to go home and he'd call when he was done. Patty knew it was about the blonde. He was out of options, so he went with the one he could understand: Clarissa.

He walked into the courthouse, where they directed him to her office. It was on the third floor at the end of the hall. Damien was expecting a cookie cutter copy of the mayor's office. He was pleasantly surprised. Clarissa's waiting room was twice as large with a secretary who looked as though she was as old as time with her black horn-rimmed glasses on.

The floor was covered in a rich blue carpet, and there was a tea and coffee station off to the side for guests as well. If Damien thought the waiting room was lush, Clarissa's office was just as if not more so. It was a large office with pictures of Clarissa on the walls. The carpet continued into the room, and there was a sitting space away from her mahogany desk and large leather chair.

"Mr. Tyler, we meet again. What do you want?"

"You know that's one of the reasons I'm here, because of your no-nonsense way of addressing things."

Clarissa smiled and led Damien over to the sitting area. Damien noticed when she sat down on the leather couch, it didn't make a sound. That was the sound of Italian leather. The flowers on the small table in front of the sofa were fresh, and Clarissa was looking at him as if she were the cat about to have a tasty meal.

"Thank you for seeing me," Damien said.

Clarissa held up her hand. "I hope you don't think the invitation to the couch is a sign of anything. I personally like to be entertained on my couch; it gives me the leeway to fall over laughing from the foolishness that I hear."

Damien nodded and kept his smile tight.

"So, Mr. Tyler, how are you liking Sweet Blooms?" Clarissa asked.

"I have to tell you that I didn't think I'd be here long enough to make an opinion about whether I liked it or not."

"I presume this isn't a social visit, so what would you like from me, Mr. Tyler? Gas money to help you on your way? Or a ticket to the nearest airport?"

Damien gritted his teeth. He wouldn't be in this situation if Patty would get his head back in the game.

"Patrick won't see me. I've been to the house several times, and he isn't as focused on the task of getting back to his business. I'm out of options. You seem like a reasonable businesswoman, so I'm here to get your assistance."

"And you thought I would assist you because?"

Damien had to consciously stop his hands from clenching. How could a deal that was so basic go so wrong? He was groveling at the feet of a beauty queen in a small town.

"You expressed an interest in keeping your people safe. Patty and I have some dealings with people that might not be as patient as he thinks. You know how things can be with money."

He saw her eyes narrow and then she leaned back in her chair and stared at him until he thought he would jump out of his seat. He didn't like her blatantly sizing him up, and he felt like whatever she was seeing, she found him lacking in some way.

"How long have you and Patrick been partners?" Clarissa asked.

"We've been together for ten plus years. He's never just up and left like this."

"Why now, Mr. Tyler? Why did he need to leave this time?"

Damien thought about not telling the truth, but his gut counseled otherwise.

"We were investing in a risky deal. It went south and needs more money so we can be there when it turns around. When it went south, we had all of our assets tied to it."

"It seems foolish to risk it all."

Damien leaned forward. "It's a sure bet. We just need to ride this low point."

"So you're gamblers?"

"Investors. Listen, I want to leave like you want me gone. We need the money from this land to do it. He says the board won't budge on the ruling. You're on the board. I'm hoping you can help me out."

Damien sat on the edge of the couch and waited. If Clarissa didn't help him out, he wasn't sure what else he would do. Clarissa got up and went to sit at her desk.

"I'll call the board together to see if we can reconsider."

Damien let the smile out but didn't jump for joy the way he felt. Instead, he stood up and went to offer his hand to Clarissa. "Thank you."

She looked at his hand and then back at him.

"You can leave, Mr. Tyler. Our business is done."

Damien dropped his hand and gave her a nod. She could say what she wanted. As long as she got the land back, he and Patty would get the money, and that's all that mattered.

"Lemonade for the lady," Patrick said, pouring from the glass pitcher.

Daisy looked around the cabin and saw that it had been cleaned and a couple of items she would have sworn were not in the place before were present.

"What, did you hire a bunch of cleaning ladies and movers to get this done?"

"The first rule about couples is that physical attraction may pique the interest, but there has to be some substance. Eating at each other's home or favorite restaurant gives clues to the other person on what kind of partner they will make."

Daisy had made it to Patrick's house on time. She was greeted with fixed steps and a painted porch. It still creaked when she stepped on it, but it looked sturdy and neat. When he opened the door, she saw throw rugs in the walkway. The walkway opened up to the living room, and off to the side of the living room, a nook had been made by having a large rug and a table placed atop that rug. The table was square and cozy for them both to sit at.

She had been trying to distract herself all day knowing she was going to do a couple's thing. Why had she thought scheduling things and knowing when they were going to happen would take away the anxiety? Having a heads up just gave her enough time to get wound up over what was coming.

"So what should I be getting from this?"

"I am a man of my word. I invited you to my cleaned up place. I didn't expect you to give me a pass on my place because I just got here or that it wasn't mine. I take care of things around me. I also wasn't sure if you wanted to eat dinner or not."

Daisy held up her hand to stop him. "I know this may not be the most romantic thing to say, but my stomach is so knotted right now, I'm afraid I couldn't keep a thing down."

Patrick smiled. "Like I was saying, I have some dinner we can heat up, or I have some light pastries we can have with the lemonade. I'm told they are light biscuits from Sweet Blooms Café that are really popular."

Daisy smiled. "You can't go wrong with items from there. Not now, maybe later. I didn't want you to go out of your way for me."

"We're a couple. This isn't out of the way. It's my way of saying I would like to spend time with you."

Daisy nodded. "Like those birds that bring an offering of grubs to potential mates."

Patrick laughed. "I can safely say no woman has ever compared going on a date with me to a grub and a bird." He went into the kitchen and brought out the box of desserts. After setting up a small plate for them both and they both took a pastry, she looked him over.

"These are amazing."

"Then I guess the lady likes my grub," he said with a smile. When they both had finished eating, Daisy pushed the plate away and waited.

"So are we done?"

"With desserts, yes. I thought we'd do some dancing."

Daisy shook her head. "No, I don't do that. I'm not musically inclined."

Patrick stood up and went to the end table next to the couch and turned on slow music.

"You don't need to have any musical inclinations. This type of music is all swaying and following. The most important thing is for you to go with the flow."

"Funny how all of this comes back to you leading the way."

"Total coincidence."

He offered his hand, and she took it. He placed his hand on her hip, and they started to sway.

"It's customary for the woman to dole out compliments for the evening if she likes them," Patrick said while smiling.

"Really?" she replied as she tried not to laugh. "Do you need some reassurance?"

"You should know men and women need reassurance from their partners. It needs to go both ways. I'm trying to provide a safe place, some food, and to help you relax with me. You would be amazed how much thought went into it."

She looked into his eyes and said, "You've provided a juicy grub today, good job."

Patrick laughed and pulled her closer in his embrace. "I don't know how romantic that was, but I'll take it."

She leaned back and looked at him, smiling. "I have my own brand of romantic. It'll grow on you, get it? Gardner…grow on you?"

He laughed at the joke. "That was horrible."

"Ah, it was, but you laughed anyway!"

"So it seems as though the gardner is a jokester?"

Daisy shrugged. "Maybe. I like the corny jokes, but I try not to torture anyone but Hannah with them."

The music stopped, and Patrick looked down at Daisy.

"It's no torture at all. Daisy, I'm going to kiss you."

She looked up and saw his eyes focused on her mouth.

"Okay."

When his head began to lower, she closed her eyes and thought of the setting sun in the evening. She thought she would be able to process the feelings and emotions easier since she knew what was happening, but she was wrong.

His lips were like butterfly wings teasing hers. A brush here and then nothing. When his lips brushed hers again, she squeezed his shoulders. It was a tease that threw her body into overdrive. As if from nowhere, a little ball of heat formed in the pit of her stomach and tingles radiated from her shoulders to her fingertips. What started as an insignificant spark grew into a wave of sensation as he pressed his lips to hers. Everything was magnified. The feel of his shoulders beneath her hands was sturdier, and the way her hands flexed as if she were trying to release some of the energy was falling into the same rhythm she felt undulating through her body. Lost in sensation, she knew there was more, and she leaned into him. His hands dropped to her hips; she felt him flex his hands at her hip, and then he broke the contact.

It took a moment for her to realize he wasn't going to come back, and she opened her eyes.

"Patrick?" she asked breathlessly. He closed his eyes and then he took a step back.

"I think it's time I took you home."

The words were like ice to her. She had been a fool. She had been worried about other people laughing at her, but no, she should have been worried about making a fool of herself in front of him.

He reached out and tilted her chin up. She blinked back the tears and tried to step away.

"Stop thinking and answering for me when I'm right here."

"There's nothing to say."

"I stopped the kiss because you came for dinner and desserts, not for me to take advantage of you."

His words sunk in, but she wasn't sure she believed them.

"I'm a grown person, Patrick. I can make my own decisions." She went from hurt to angry in seconds.

"Daisy, please. What kind of partner would I be if I didn't look out for you? Don't be mad because I'm thinking of you. You are not the issue. We are not ready, and I got caught up in the kiss more than I thought I would."

She looked at him, and he began to speak, but she silenced him with her fingers on his lips.

"You're right. I don't have to like it, but I'll admit you're right. Thank you," she said softly to him.

"May I walk you home?"

She smiled at him. "I'd be delighted."

The walk beneath the stars was the perfect end to her first kiss.

Twelve

"We want to thank Daisy for appraising the new land lots that were submitted to our committee. As usual, Daisy was very diligent in making sure the size of the acreage was right so we can issue the voting ballots to owners of ten acres or more of farmable land," Agnes said. She nodded to Daisy. "How many of them were shocked their land wasn't as valuable as they thought it was?"

Daisy sighed. "It's always a shock to people who have lived on the land for a while but haven't been using it to make a profit how much money is needed to get it ready. I don't like being the bearer of bad news to anyone. This is just so we can function as a voting board. We all agreed the largest landowners should have a voice when speaking."

"That sounds like there were indeed some disappointed people," another member of the committee said with a grin.

"I don't want people to dread when I come to their property," Daisy moaned.

"No, it's fine. If you didn't, we'd be going through hundreds of petitions, but now we only need to go through two."

Agnes was the head of the Land Committee. The Land Committee took proposals to the largest landowners for approval with construction, real estate, and new business projects. It was an effort created by Robert Morgan to make sure the landowners weren't shut off due to the new renovations and improvements being done.

They reviewed a claim by Skye O'Malley first.

"We are looking at the Skye O'Malley's claim. Now that she's the owner of her land, her family's land, and her brother's, she's asked for membership. Let's vote," Agnes said.

All of the hands went up. What made the process easy was the committee usually accepted Daisy's evaluation. With Skye's application approved, they moved on to the next one.

"Well, well, look at this. A Patrick Cunningham has applied for membership. Now that he's the official owner of the land and it's been evaluated, he qualifies."

Daisy raised her hand because she wanted to speak to the application.

"I wanted everyone to know that I live on the land, but I did assess it, and I provided the numbers that were used by the last independent assessment. In both cases, the land is salvageable, and he has over ten acres."

"I reviewed the assessment," Agnes said. "I think this case is a little more complex."

"It's true, he's not Carl. How can we let this city man on the committee? He's probably a plant to get us to do what a big-time realtor wants," said another member on the committee.

"It's true, he's from the city and not from Sweet

Blooms; inheriting property doesn't mean you really want to do anything."

Daisy heard the conversation, and a moment of shame came over her. She had expressed these same ideas to some degree. Now that she knew him, that she had given him a chance, she knew that he was more and deserved better.

"I know Patrick is new, but I think it's important that we look at what he's done while he's been here since we don't have any history on him before."

"We can all imagine what he was doing before. I think in view of the kind of person he is, we have no choice but to say no or to push this application off for further review."

Daisy hadn't planned on it, but she spoke up and said: "You can't be serious?"

Everyone in the room turned towards her and looked to her as if there was something wrong with her.

"Daisy, I'm a little surprised that you have a problem with this. He may look good, and he may say all the right things now, but that's what these city guys do. They do and say whatever it is they need to do now in order to get their way."

"I guess I don't get it, Agnes. What exactly are we denying his application for? Are we saying no because he wasn't born in Sweet Blooms? Are we saying no because he has shown some characteristic that only city people have? Let's say I was open to that theory. What is that characteristic? Did he comply with all of the rules to put in his application?"

"Yes, he did, but—"

Daisy looked at Agnes, who looked around at the other women.

"Fine, if you want it spelled out, then I can do it," Agnes said.

"Okay, what is it?"

"He's not dependable. He's a city guy, and to allow him to make decisions is a mistake because he won't be here long enough to see them manifested."

"You know that because?"

The other women looked at Agnes, and then she looked back at Daisy.

"If it's important to you, we will accept his application, but mark my words, he'll act just like all the other city people. He'll live in Sweet Blooms and think it's a great place and then he'll have ideas on how to change it. When he can't change it to fit the ideal he has in his head, he'll leave. They all leave to go back to the city."

"You had to hear them talk about Patrick like they knew him," Daisy said as she clipped the ends of the new plants. "I was waiting for someone to say they knew how he was going to act because it was on Cops Live. It was surreal to hear them judge him based on where he came from. How could this happen in Sweet Blooms?"

Hannah was sitting on the other side of the table, and she rapped her knuckles on the table.

"It wasn't so long ago those same biases were applied to your mother. A single woman with a child living out there with Carl Cunningham. They don't come into town, and you know the rumors flew for years. Sweet Blooms is a town like any other. Maybe you should put the shears down before some plant suffers your indignation."

Daisy shook her head as she placed the mini shears to the side.

"I would never take out my frustration on a helpless plant. These came in today, and I want to make sure they stay healthy, so a little snip from the bottom of the stalks is what is in order. Not enough to send them into shock but enough to make sure the dead end is removed."

Daisy looked at Hannah, smiling.

"What was I talking about before?"

"You were being indignant for Patrick. I think you're right, but remember that Patrick is just the latest news. He's attractive, new, and unknown. That makes him ripe for those who have no lives."

"I know you're right, but the injustice of it all caught me unaware."

"It seems like Patrick has caught you unaware."

Daisy continued to pick up the clipped pieces of stem.

"It's not what you think. I was moved because it was so similar to my own situation of being judged by others without anyone even bothering to get to know me or ask me a thing."

Hannah held her hands up in defense.

"I can see the similarities, but I want to talk to you as a friend. Patrick is an unknown and I don't want you to get hurt."

"We have an understanding, and we're friends."

"That's it?"

"That's all that matters. I'm not deluding myself thinking that Patrick and I are going to do the happily ever after move. I help him, and he helps me, that's it."

Hannah switched the subject to the flowers she wanted at her wedding and asked what would be a fair price. After an hour, she left, and Daisy was alone with her thoughts.

Daisy valued Hannah as a friend and knew she was concerned about her and Patrick being something more. Daisy, on the other hand, wasn't concerned at all. She understood that Patrick was just keeping to their deal. When their time was over, they would both be able to say there was a fair exchange.

Damien knew his time was running out and he had to attack this problem from several directions. One of those directions brought him to flower keeper's front door. He rang the bell and waited. He'd seen her truck outside and had touched the hood; it was still warm. She was here, and she was home.

He had been all through the town sitting in little stores and shops. It wasn't until he met an older woman named Agnes that he was able to get some history on Daisy. He was going to change the approach and see if he could help things along. Hearing Patty had applied for and become a part of the land committee was enough to galvanize him into action. It was clear to him that Patty had lost his focus.

Damien knocked on the door this time, and within minutes, the door was opened.

"I told you I was coming," she said, a bit out of breath. "My hands were dirty from planting some new shoots."

"Shoots?"

"I received some baby plants, and they needed to be planted as soon as I unpacked them. So I heard you, but they took precedence. What can I do for you, Mr. Tyler?"

"I thought we could talk. I'm in town for a couple of days, and the only other person I know is Patty, who's very busy these days. Do you mind?"

Daisy stepped back and let him in. She motioned for him to take a seat on the couch. Damien looked at the interior; it was homey. It had those touches of a woman who spent time alone: knitted blankets with nature themes, plaques on the wall that said Bless This House. No pictures of children or family.

"You've got a good eye with the house," he said as he sat down on the oversized couch. "I'm a little surprised there aren't more flowers or plants in your place."

Daisy stood by the couch and crossed her arms over her chest. She was still in a tee shirt and blue jeans.

"Did you come to talk to me, Mr. Tyler, or to criticize my home and how it doesn't meet your expectations of a gardner?"

"I'm sorry, please forgive me. It's an occupational hazard, nothing more." Damien knew he had to be careful. He thought about everything he knew about Daisy and started again.

Daisy took a seat across from him and waited.

Damien could see why Patty was distracted. Any other time he'd encourage him to indulge, but money was in the mix now, and things had to change, and quickly.

"You said it was an occupational hazard," Daisy said, breaking the silence.

"Yes, Patty and I assess the value of things and then take calculated risks."

"You assess the value of things?"

"Yes, well, let me tell you the story. Patty and I grew up in the same neighborhood. We had a light touch and swift feet even when we were young."

Daisy looked confused. "A light touch?"

Damien smiled and then cleared his throat. "I'm sorry for using the euphemisms. When we were smaller, we would shoplift and not get caught. We grew up in a poor neighborhood."

Damien watched the horror and shock spread across Daisy's face. Holding his hands up, he said emphatically, "We don't lift today. Those were our beginnings. We graduated from that to casinos and poker tables. Patty's really good about reading numbers and probability. When we hit our twenties, we went to work for the stock market and used all of our skills to become traders."

"Like on the stock market?"

"Yes, just like that. Patty's got a reputation for being able to pick a stock that's a real winner. He tried to do it recently, and he called it wrong, but I'm sure he'll get it back."

"That's why he came to Sweet Blooms? To get the money to go back?"

Damien nodded. "Yes, it is, but it seems like there are a lot more rules in liquidating the land than he originally thought. I know the two of you have been working on it, and that's why Patty is so busy."

Daisy looked at Damien, and her mouth twitched, and the corners dared to curl upwards.

"Wow, Mr. Tyler, you must think I'm very naïve for you come here with your story."

"No, no, of course not. Quite the contrary."

"Mr. Tyler, I think you should leave." Daisy stood up and went to her door and held it open. Damien stood up, unsure. He wasn't sure what had happened, and the confusion must have shown on his face.

"You're wondering why I'm showing you the door? One, you came here under false pretenses. You aren't lonely or need someone to talk to. You thought by telling me these things about Patrick that I'd do… what? Not talk to him or maybe not help him? Patrick was honest with me. He told me he wasn't a good person, Mr. Tyler. He didn't give me the details, but he didn't keep it from me.

I have to think that if you're the kind of friend that Patrick has in the city, it's no wonder he's willing to take his time here in Sweet Blooms. We may not be the most advanced or open minded people, but you know where you stand with us all.

Good day to you, Mr. Tyler."

Damien realized he had pushed too hard and Patty had beat him to the punch.

"I didn't mean to offend. Perhaps we'll be able to talk again later."

"Good day, Mr. Tyler."

Thirteen

"I thought I had a problem making friends," Daisy said as she sliced up the hero Patrick had brought over. "He comes to my door like the wicked witch bearing a shiny red apple."

Patrick just looked at her as she recalled her meeting with Damien. It was just the two of them, and he had been here before, but now hearing her tell the story, this meeting seemed momentous.

"Daisy, I have to ask you something."

"Go ahead," she said as she took a large bite out of her sandwich.

"When he was talking, were you upset or shocked by what he said?"

She wiped the back of her hand over her mouth and stopped chewing for a moment. Then she shook her head and swallowed.

"No, we had already talked about it, and I don't need to know your past, Patrick. I'm not some confessor or even someone who can pass judgment on you. I can only go by what you give me today. Maybe those things happened. I can't be angry at them or say you were a horrible person. Do you know why?"

"No. I have to tell you I'm confused. I don't know that I would have taken the information as well."

Daisy laughed. "Well, I guess it's a good thing that I didn't have even half the exciting childhood that you had."

Patrick laughed, but he came back to the subject. He felt like he was at some hill or precipice. The words she said now mattered.

"Daisy, answer the question for me because I have to tell you I'm beyond curious. Why weren't you angry or at least upset about my past?"

"Patrick, everything that you went through in the past has made you the man you are today. I like the man you are today, so I can't begrudge the boy you were yesterday."

Her words stopped him in his tracks. He froze in his seat and just looked at her. Unbidden, she had given him her faith. She hadn't asked him to defend his past or made him feel bad about it. He thought about all the times people had judged him because of where he had come from and what he had done.

As if sensing the change in his attitude, she pushed another section of the sandwich towards him. "I wouldn't worry about your past. At least you can say you were young. I have no excuse for how rude I was to Mr. Tyler. I hope he just goes away."

Patrick wanted to explain to her. He wanted to make her understand that she was the first person to not care about his past. She was the first person to give him a go despite what he had done. He wasn't sure how he was going to make her understand the gift she had given him, but he'd find a way.

"What does your gut tell you about that hope?" Patrick asked.

"It says I'm going to be out of luck. But I'm hoping that I don't have to rely on that because I've been batting a thousand against my gut."

"Okay, you know you have to explain that comment."

Sighing, Daisy pushed away the rest of the sandwich.

"Recently, the business has been picking up. When I get personal requests, I have to close the shop to go."

"Sounds good so far."

"It is. Hannah suggested I get some help. I put out an ad, and I got an overwhelming response. I finally narrowed it down to two candidates. One of them is a young woman who is very computer savvy but doesn't know flowers. The other candidate knows flowers, and I know the woman as well. The issue is she admits that computers are a challenge for her."

"That's a tough call to make. What did your gut say?"

"The older woman."

"Why didn't you listen to your gut?"

"I didn't listen because my first private party is coming up, and if I had taken on the other candidate, I wouldn't have had time to train her on the computers. I didn't want to set her up to fail, so I chose the other one."

Patrick stood up and cleared off the table.

"The good news is, if you have made the wrong choice, you can always go back and ask the other candidate if they'd like the job."

Daisy started laughing.

"What's so funny?"

"You may have this couple thing down, but you

don't know women if you think I could go back and offer the second woman the job."

Patrick put his hand to his chest in mock pain.

"Ow, did she take a jab at me and doubt my skills all at the same time? Haven't I shown you the basics of couples? You've made sure I'm a good person. We've shared a meal, so you know I have patience and can provide for you. We only have two more couple things to do, and then you'll be a graduate of couple basics 101."

"Two more things, you say, and I'll get my certificate?"

Patrick laughed.

"That's right, so let's go do one of them now."

Daisy's eyes lit up. "Okay."

"You need to go change into your bathing suit."

"My bathing suit? Why don't I change when I get there? If there is a pool, they have lockers. I'll change there."

Patrick shook his head. "Come on, give me a little more of your trust, and I promise you, you won't be disappointed."

Daisy looked at him as if he were crazy, but finally, she relented.

"I'll be back in ten, and then we can go."

True to her word, she was dressed in a blue and yellow one-piece bathing suit. When he said they had to walk there, she put on a pair of shorts and a top.

"I don't have to tell you how silly I feel doing this, Patrick."

"I don't have to tell you how curious I am about your bathing suit. You do know there is a parrot on the back of the suit?"

She smiled. "I do. It was a joke purchase between Hannah and me. I told her I didn't want anyone looking at me too long before I get into the pool. So this bathing suit makes them all look at other parts of me so I can get into the pool without feeling self-conscious."

Patrick laughed. "I can see how you thought this was going to be a good idea. I can also tell you that it does distract a person from looking at you, but only for a moment. No matter what you did, there is no way to hide; you are a beautiful woman."

Daisy smiled and didn't comment. They continued to walk when Daisy broke the silence.

"What is that?"

Patrick knew what she was seeing. He had put up an outdoor canopy tent. Underneath it, he had laid out two lounge chairs, a small metal table with lemonade, and an inflatable pool. As she got closer, he saw her eyes light up.

"Oh my goodness, come on!" Daisy grabbed his hand and pulled him along with her as she got to the tent. He watched her go from one item to another. It was like watching Goldilocks in real time. He'd had some doubts when he first thought of it. Looking at her laughing and going from chair to chair, he realized it was all worth it.

"I take it you like it?" he asked.

"Like you even need to ask! Come join me."

He went to the chair and started to take his shirt off.

"What are you doing?" she asked.

He looked at her, and the once smiling woman was gone.

"Daisy, I have my swimming trunks on under here."

Her smile came back, and she nodded. "Ah, no problem. Go right ahead. How did you get the pool up and out here anyway?"

"It's not permanent, and don't lean on the sides; it's a blowup pool. I actually rented it from the community center."

When he noticed her rambling, he turned his back to her and then took off his pants. He knew what would happen next. He heard her giggling. He had prepared for this. From the back, it was the rear end of a raccoon's tail. The front wouldn't be any easier.

He looked over his shoulder to see her bent over in laughter.

"You know, it's not like I travel with swimming trunks, so I had to find what would work for me. What that really means is I found a size that would fit and, go figure, it looked like these were amongst the ones that were left. I had a choice between the raccoon or a bunny, and I couldn't do the bunny tail."

Daisy couldn't comment; she was sitting on the end of the lounge chair trying to keep from laughing. When he turned around, she saw the front of the picture. It was a raccoon with large glasses holding a mason jar of liquid.

"It looks adorable!"

Patrick shook his head. "I have to tell you when a man stands in front of an attractive woman in his swimming trunks, he never imagines she'll say he looks adorable."

Wiping the errant tears from her eyes, she looked him in the eye.

"I'm ready to go to the pool now."

Sighing in indignation, he gave her a smile to let her know he was okay with the ribbing. He stepped over the two-foot plastic wall into the water. Then he reached out his hand.

"Come, come in, my fair princess. I've made sure there are no dangers lurking in the pool."

Daisy laughed. "The pool isn't big enough to have anything lurking in it."

Patrick put his hand over his heart. "That doesn't make my deed any less chivalrous. Come, come, the mere sight of me is fending off the monsters."

Daisy took his hand, and they both sat in the water. The pool was long enough for them to lay in it as long as they were both laying in the same direction. After Daisy got into the pool, she sighed.

"The water is a welcome relief to the day's heat."

After sitting in silence for ten minutes, Patrick broke the silence.

"Couples don't always spend money and go to extravagant places. Sometimes the best memories are made close to home."

Daisy nodded. "I know nothing could be truer than that statement. I will never in a million years forget your raccoon trunks."

Patrick snorted. "You aren't off the hook either with memorable swimwear. Really, a parrot on your back?"

Just as it seemed she was about to reply, they both heard a phone. The ring tone was *Here Comes the Bride.*

"Oh, no, not now!" Daisy said as she tried to get out of the pool. When she turned in the pool, her legs tangled with Patrick's, and when she instinctively pulled her legs back, she leaned against the wall of the pool, and it began to sag under her weight.

"You need to answer the phone?"

"Yes, it's the shop. I'm expecting a special delivery."

Finally, she managed to push herself up by leaning on Patrick to get out of the pool. She reached for her phone, and Patrick stood up, listening to what was going to be the end of his night.

"No, no, it's no problem you called me, Tate," Daisy said.

He saw her nod her head a couple more times, and then she hung up.

She looked at Patrick with regret and hesitation in her eyes.

"I've got to go. Hannah's flowers have arrived."

Patrick got out of the pool and reached off to the side for towels. He wrapped her in one of the fluffy white towels.

"I know you have a business; it's no problem."

"I feel bad that I'm leaving the pool and your planning and—"

"Couples have all the time in the world. These moments and surprises make the moments special. Now come on, I'll walk you home so you can go to the shop. I think Hannah is a nice person, but if I get in the way of her flowers for her wedding, I'm afraid I'll see a whole new side of her."

Fourteen

The next morning Patrick called and asked her if she would have coffee and snacks with him at the coffee house.

"I'm thinking we can go to the tea and coffee place in town," he said.

"I think we should go to Sweet Blooms Cafe for all of that," Daisy suggested.

"Normally, I would agree, but this is part of our couples thing. It's the final and most important step."

"And that is?"

"Being in public. I think we're good when it comes to being with each other. We know each other and trust each other as well. All that is needed when we face the public together."

"You make it sound like we're going to war. This is Sweet Blooms."

Patrick clicked his teeth.

"Don't let the quiet towns fool you. They are the first ones to cause drama and break up couples who aren't strong in the force. The only thing more powerful than well-meaning neighbors is family! Da-da-da-dum."

"Enough with you already!" she said, laughing.

"I'll see you at two, then. You'll recognize me—"

"Yes, you'll be the guy with the fat ego and raccoon trunks," she said and hung up the phone.

At two o'clock on the dot, she had called Tate in to take over, and she had made it to the shop. She almost fell over laughing when she saw there was a plush raccoon on the circular metal table.

"I ordered some coffee and biscuits. The biscuits won't be to die for like the ones from Sweet Blooms Cafe, but they'll get you through the day," Patrick said.

"So you just happen to have a stuffed raccoon in your car," she said, as she sat across from him at the table. "You must have an assortment of animals in your car."

Patrick smiled. "How did you know. I meant to bring the parrot, but I thought for our first outing, this would be enough."

Daisy's pulse jumped when he said for the first outing. That was the sign that she was heading towards trouble.

"I want you to know I have this raccoon for you. I didn't want to wave like an idiot, and I guarantee that when you saw this little guy, you knew exactly where I was sitting. It was an ingenious plan."

Daisy leaned forward. "So what you're telling me is the women you normally date aren't the brightest crayons in the bunch. They smile a lot like a toothpaste commercial but don't really talk."

"Ow. Again, you've taken aim and scored hitting my heart," he said. Then the waitress came with their order.

Just as Patrick planned, they were at the local coffee spot, sitting on the sidewalk. The awning provided minimal shade, and the occasional breeze did nothing but move the hot air around. True to Patrick's prediction, people were everywhere. When she looked up, she could catch people looking at her and quickly looking away. This is what Patrick called the final test. She thought he had been exaggerating, but now she could see this was completely different.

He knew they needed to have some history of being comfortable with one another to be able to ignore the others who were beyond nosy. What did she know about Patrick? He was smart, funny, considerate, but most of all, he was human. He admitted his faults and didn't try to hide from them.

She looked at him smiled, and for a moment, the question came unbidden to her mind. Why was this the trial run and not the real thing?

"Hey, you, stop thinking over there. I have to tell you the rules," Patrick whispered in a hushed voice.

"Why are you whispering?"

Patrick smiled. "To make you lean your head down a little closer to mine. When you do that, it makes it seems like we are talking about something very intimate."

Daisy laughed but peeked at the other people who seemed to be looking at them more and more.

"You see, the other part of being a couple in public is that you and that person have managed to create your own space and secrets even though you are outside. You wanted me to show you what it's like to be a part of the town. If you think about it, you'll be able to say people have talked to you more and wanted to come into the shop more. Part of that is because you are part of a couple and they want to know what is it that I find so interesting about you that they missed."

Daisy looked into his eyes as he was speaking and realized Patrick had done so much for her already. She was at a point now where she didn't know where her friend started and where he was just fulfilling his part. Every morning they had been looking at the crops and then discussing which herbs she grew when and why. He was as attentive on the land as he was sitting at the table.

It seemed like a big part of being a part of the town was making sure you knew who you were first.

"Now, to make sure everyone knows we're a couple when you leave, make sure you take the raccoon."

Daisy looked at the toy.

"Really?"

"When you do, I bet you there will be at least three tales that start to circulate. The first will be you're expecting. The second will be we had a fight, but I made it up to you, and the third will be I'm trying to get back in your good graces."

"So you seem to know what's going on and how everyone will act. Is this a regular thing you do with your women of preference?" she teased.

"No, I can say this is strictly a Daisy event."

"Is this a private party or can anyone join?"

Daisy heard Damien's voice and closed her eyes. She knew that wouldn't help. Damien wouldn't just get up and leave no matter how much she wanted him to.

She opened her eyes and found Damien was sitting down at the table with a smile on his face as if he'd been invited to the table. To add insult to injury, when the waitress went by, he flagged her down and ordered an iced tea.

"Hello, Patty."

"Hello, Damien."

"It seems that since you found your young lady here, you don't have time for your old friends."

Patrick smiled at Daisy. "Did it occur to you that I hadn't forgotten you? I was just making new friends."

Damien's voice became strained and tight.

"In a town this small, you can't keep avoiding me."

Patrick turned his attention to Damien.

"I don't need to try to avoid you. I have work to do."

"You came here to unload some land, and now you have work to do?"

Daisy listened to the two men go back and forth, and it was a surreal experience. It was like a tennis match when both people were evenly matched.

"I need you to wrap this deal up, Patty. There are people who need to get paid."

"What are you talking about, Damien? Everything I had was repossessed or sold to pay off what I owed. I left with nothing to my name but the five thousand I had in my house."

"We made a plan, Patty. I bought an item or two based on the money you'd get. Some of that money is mine as well, you know?"

Daisy had to interrupt. "I don't think you can borrow on stuff that's not yours, and the land Patrick has isn't really his. It's always been a town rule to really let people stay free of charge on the land."

Damien looked at Daisy, and she felt chilled by his glare. Then he shifted his glare back to Patrick.

"And who is the woman all of a sudden, Patty?"

Patrick laid his hand out palm up. Without giving it a second thought, she put her hand in his. Patrick smiled and then looked at Damien.

"We're a couple."

The words she had been dreaming about had been spoken. Obviously, this couldn't be true. She knew he was saying it to save face in front of Damien, but the words were still powerful. Patrick was all the things she knew he was, and kind to boot.

Damien gave them both a once over and then chuckled before reaching out to give a slight punch to Patrick's shoulder. The sound was low and muffled as he looked around the café. Daisy could tell he thought it was a joke at best. At that moment, Daisy was once again on the outskirts looking in. She was the only child with no family. She was the daughter with no dad. The person no one wanted to dance with and the one that everyone knew was different. She waited for Patrick's confession that they weren't really a couple. That he was trying to teach her how to be normal.

Patrick picked up his coffee cup and then decided to add sugar. "Your sense of humor was always beyond me, so I have to ask, Damien, what are you snickering at?"

"You and the blonde? Knowing what's waiting for us, how could you even entertain being with her?"

Just when Daisy thought it couldn't get any worse, it did. She looked down into her coffee cup and wrapped her hands around the mug. She could blink away the tears, and no one would see. She was actually really good at blinking away tears. The warm, errant wind helped her to keep her composure. She just hoped Patrick was kind in his comment.

"The only reason you are saying things like that is because you haven't really lived in Sweet Blooms or gotten to know Daisy to understand what makes her the better option," Patrick said. Patrick reached across the table and grabbed Daisy's hand in his.

"Daisy is unlike any woman I've met. She is a combination of the all-knowing earth mother and a carefree child. She's honest, beautiful on the inside and outside, and giving to everyone she meets. More importantly, she doesn't mind telling me when I'm wrong. She's the woman that you didn't even notice was a necessary part of your life."

Daisy knew he was defending her. She knew this was part of the last lesson of being a couple, but that didn't stop her from soaking in the words. It didn't stop her dreaming that one day someone would say those words and mean them. He had chosen things about her character that everyone could see.

Damien sat back in his chair and looked between the both of them and then at their entwined hands. "It seems that I don't know you as well as I thought, Patty, or should I say Patrick?" Damien stood up and gave Daisy a nod and then left.

Daisy could feel the eyes of everyone in the café looking at them.

"Do you think that was the best thing to do? You two are friends."

"We may have been friends, but we two are a couple. Couple trumps friend in this case."

"He's waiting for his friend to come back to him."

"He's waiting for a free ride to show up and make things freer and easier for him."

Patrick squeezed her hand.

"Come on, beautiful, let me see those brown eyes," he coaxed.

She looked up and lifted her head at the same time.

"You are beautiful, kind, and considerate. I am amazed by your strength and insight. Damien is looking out for Damien. I know you don't think so, but you have so many people here in Sweet Blooms who are rooting for you. Think about the response you got when you put an ad out. You must be trusted and accepted as part of the community."

"I guess I am," she whispered. "I think I can accept that now, but in the beginning, I thought a lot of the people spoke to me because Hannah was my friend. Patrick, maybe your friend is the same. He doesn't know if people like him or who he hangs out with."

Patrick brought her hand to his lips.

"Again, you are being more kind to him than he would be to you."

"Patrick."

"Okay, he may be here out of a sense of desperation. He did tell me he's getting older and he wanted to do one more big score."

"I don't know about the next big score, but you can be there to help him if he really wants it."

Patrick looked at his watch.

"Our time is almost up. I have just enough time to get you back to work. I'm sorry for the interruption. I wanted you to have some eats and then maybe talk about the people around you and how they all want to be you—young, beautiful, and single. Right now you could have your pick of the litter, so to speak."

Daisy listened to Patrick as they went home, but she was still in the moment where he held her hand and told her all the reasons he thought she was great. It wasn't real, but for that moment she could imagine that he really meant it and she and Patrick were a couple.

Fifteen

Daisy understood there were some people who you couldn't save, and then there were some people who needed someone to give them a helping hand. When she thought about Damien, she was upset that he had exposed her weakness, but later on that night, she felt bad for him. He was alone. He needed money for whatever it was he was doing, and he had stayed with Patrick for some time. While sympathy was high, she decided to try to reach out to him and invite him for tea. Now, as the hour approached, she contemplated staying in her house and being very, very quiet.

It was noon when he showed up. Daisy went to the door, took a deep breath, and then opened it.

"Hello, Damien," she said. "I've set up a table outside since it's a cool day." She thought she saw his smile tighten for a moment, but when she looked again, it was gone, and she thought she must have let her nerves push her to start imagining things.

"Of course, Daisy."

Damien was dressed in jeans and a plaid shirt. Somehow the shirt had perfect creases in it, and the jeans looked as though they had been pressed.

The complete look should have made him look like he belonged in Sweet Blooms, but in the end, it made him look like he had stepped out of a store window. Even the gift bag he had matched his ensemble. It was a plaid blue and black bag.

Daisy had on a sundress, and looking at how crisp he was dressed, she wished she had worn something that looked casually beautiful. When she thought about her sunflower yellow dress and the green flip flops she had on, she shook her head at how typically unkept she must look.

Damien had pulled out the other chair and waited until she sat down. He put the bag on the table. "A peace offering to make up for my behavior yesterday," he said. "It doesn't excuse anything, but I'm hoping you'll accept it in the vein that it is meant."

"Thank you. I have tea, and I can bring out a coffee pot if you want it."

"No, tea is fine."

Daisy poured the two cups of tea. She had brought out her best china for the occasion. It was white and blue china cups. After filling the cups and then giving him the sugar bowl, she prepared their tea and they looked at each other. Damien broke the silence.

"Well, this is a bit awkward. I have to confess this is the first time that I've been in this type of situation, so we are both in new territory here, I suppose."

Daisy nodded. "Agreed. I was hoping that we could start over and get to know each other. I think our mutual connection with Patrick should act as a bridge for us to be civil to one another."

"Agreed. I'm a little unclear about your job. Are you a florist or an herbalist? And why do that here when you could make so much more money in the city?"

"I've always been good when it comes to working with plants. My mother and I didn't have a lot of money, so growing our own herbs was a natural alternative. I was happy to find out that other people could benefit from the information that I knew. I could work in the city. I've been offered, but there is something about knowing the people and the family environment."

Damien nodded. "It must be like working in the neighborhood you grew up in. You know everyone. It must be comforting to know everyone."

"You and Patrick were in the same neighborhood?"

"Yeah, Patty and I have been together for a while. We've always done things together, and it's hard to see him here doing things without me."

"I think you can still be a part of what he's doing, but you might want to start with calling him by his name, Patrick."

"It seems so odd to do so," Damien added.

"I think Patrick will appreciate it."

"I have to ask you, are you and Patrick really a couple?"

Daisy stiffened and braced herself for the verbal attack.

"Patrick and I have found that we have some things in common."

"I'm curious, how did you two meet?"

"He's my neighbor. We aren't the kind of place to not talk to our neighbors. So I went to talk to him, and we discovered we have things in common."

Damien took another sip. "I guess I would just caution that maybe you two don't speak the same language."

"I know he grew up different. I know that, and I'm not afraid of those differences."

"I think it's more than that. Where a person grows up shapes a person. I think at the end of the day you might find the things you would never do are things he would consider. I think the both of you need to be realistic."

Daisy took a deep breath and let it out. All of her hopes that they would be able to work together were fleeting like a summer shower on a dry, muggy day.

"What are you trying to say? That we aren't really talking or connecting as a couple? That whatever this is, it's superficial?"

Damien sat back and opened his hands. "I'm saying that couples usually come from similar experiences. You would not be the kind of person I would expect him to hook up with."

Just when she thought he couldn't say anything else that would offend her, she was unpleasantly surprised. It didn't matter that it was probably true. What mattered was they were supposed to be here to make amends and find a way to co-exist for Patricks's sake.

"So I have to ask, what is it about me that you think is just not up to snuff for Patrick? Am I too country? Not refined enough?"

Damien laughed and sat back. "No, no, I don't want you to take this the wrong way. You just aren't what I would expect for Patrick. I think you are too good for him."

From anyone else, she would have taken it as a compliment, but she knew nothing good was coming from Damien.

"You think he'll take advantage of me? You think I can't be with a man like him?"

Damien reached out and patted her hand. "You've lived in this town all of your life. I can't expect you to have the skills to handle a man like Patrick."

Daisy recognized there was some truth to the statement, which made the dagger go a little deeper into her soul.

"Don't worry about me, Damien. I'm a big girl."

"I'm trying to help you out."

"How do you see that? Do you think that telling me I'm too naïve to be with Patrick is helping?"

He motioned around him with his hands. "Look around here. Do you think that working in the herbal fields helps you to deal with men like Patrick? Patrick is a perfected package. We grew up knowing every asset we had and working it. Everything from how we talk, how we walk, and how we dress. Tell me, have you ever seen him unkept? When he walks into a room, he's noticed. Do you think any of that is an accident?"

Daisy didn't answer. Instead, she heard all of her hidden fears voiced by Damien. She was the outside flower girl. She was the one no one noticed or remembered until they needed something. Patrick was larger than life. If Daisy were honest with herself, she'd have to admit if it weren't for their land being adjacent, the two of them would have never met. She had set the situation up. She was the pity case that needed help. She had all but forced him to comply.

"It wasn't like that," she murmured.

Damien pursed his lips and then clicked his tongue. Tsk, tsk, tsk. "I know it seems unfair when you look at it because I know you meant only the best, but we need to face facts. You should be with someone who has more in common with you. At the end of the day, you and

Patrick would have never met if it weren't for these circumstances."

Daisy got up and stood behind her chair. She wasn't sure if she was using it as a barrier against Damien or if she was using it to stand up.

"I think this tea is over. You can leave now, Damien."

Damien stopped and looked up at her with confusion. "I thought we understood things just fine. I thought—"

"You thought it was going fine as long as I agreed that I'm somehow less because I grew up in Sweet Blooms and I'm definitely not in Patrick's league. I was wrong, and I'm sad to say Patrick was right. You are a manipulative person who will do whatever it takes to get your way. Right now, the only focus you have is to get Patrick to leave and for us to break up as a couple. I've done my best to reach out, and now I'm satisfied with the effort. You can leave."

Damien looked at her again, incredulously. "You're really kicking me out!"

Looking around, Daisy replied. "You're not really getting kicked out. You never made it into my house. Good day."

Daisy didn't say anything as Damien left. She watched him drive away. Even after he had left her house, she didn't move until the dust had settled from the road that he had driven down. Then she took a seat at the table and laid her head on top of her folded arms. She was in so much shock she couldn't even cry. She knew it was the end; the problem was she couldn't name what she had just lost, but it was significant.

The next morning, Patrick came over just as he had every morning. Patrick knew he was running late, but he wanted to stop by and give Daisy her morning hug and coffee. When he walked in and saw her at work already, he waved to get her attention. Instead of the ready smile, she only gave him a nod. It felt odd, but Patrick nodded back. There was something off. He didn't leave; instead, he waited. When the crowd left, she walked the last customer out and put on the "I'll be back in twenty minutes" sign.

"Hey, what's up?" Patrick said, moving towards her. Daisy put her hand up and stopped him in his tracks.

"I'm glad you came. I need to talk to you," she said.

"Okay."

He noticed her body seemed tense, and she moved slower than she normally did. He knew something was wrong; he just needed to have enough patience to wait for it. Daisy didn't lie to him, so he knew she'd tell him the problem and they'd come up with an answer.

She went to the door and leaned against it. "I want to tell you that you have been amazing. I know things about couples that I never even thought of."

"I know things I never thought I knew as well." He thought that would bring a smile to her face, but it fell flat. He was getting nervous.

"Well, I'm glad that you got some benefit from this. I want to say I'll give you any help you need with the land. I'll talk to the board for you as well. I'll tell them you are working the land although I think you know enough to pass any interview they give you. What I'm saying is, I think we're done."

He stopped and looked at her and waited to see what

else she would say. When she stopped talking, he went to the counter and turned towards her.

"You decided you have learned all you need from me?"

Daisy nodded. "It was an odd deal to make from the get-go. I'm glad you even went along with it for how long you did."

"I didn't say anything."

Daisy nodded, but she wasn't looking at him. In fact, he wasn't sure that she even knew he was there. He thought he was going to move their relationship in another direction, but she wanted to end it. Didn't she realize how rare what they had was? He wasn't sure what it was, but he knew it was more than he'd had before, and until he could name it one way or another, he didn't want it to go away.

"Patrick, I can't thank you enough for all you've done. No one would have done this, and you did it without a thought," she rambled on.

"What happened, Daisy?" he asked desperately. "Who said something to move you to this decision?"

She stopped and looked him in the eye. "This is what's best. It's not about what other people think. It's about what's best for you."

"Wow, is that the story you're sticking with, because if it is, you should reconsider your story."

"Maybe that's the problem. You are way more understanding of these things than I am," she fired back.

"That was all Damien."

"Does any of that matter? Didn't we agree we could walk away when we wanted to? Well, I want to walk away. Will you keep your word to me?"

If she had asked him this question just a week ago, he would have been able to say anything it took to get her to go his way, but now, after they had shared so much, he couldn't do that to her.

It was a joke between him and Damien that he would never leave a good thing. He would say there was no situation where he would leave money on the table. All of those brave words were true before he met Daisy. Now she was asking him to honor his word. He could sway her. He could get her to change her mind, and yet, he stood still.

"Yes, I'll honor my word."

With those words, he left her and went to his car. He sat in his car and beat his steering wheel and then started his car up. This wasn't over, but he needed to think. He needed time to understand what was going on, and right now, he couldn't think beyond the haze of hurt and betrayal.

Sixteen

Daisy thought she understood pain. She thought when her mother passed away, that was the worst pain she would ever feel. She was wrong. Sometimes a person could be in so much pain they couldn't even cry. Daisy knew she was hurting, but still, there was no way for her to express the pain. She made it to her bedroom and then she got under the covers. It started with a chill that she knew she shouldn't be feeling.

The weather was always around 70, so the idea that she was cold was ridiculous. Still, she huddled under the covers. Then her stomach began to have little cramps that made her bend over. When she curled into herself, she felt something hit her head. She reached out, and her hand found the raccoon. She stroked it once and then, like a dam, she felt the burning behind the eyes and the blurring of the room.

She'd done the right thing by Patrick. As time went on, she realized that she had been wrong to get Patrick to help her out that way. He had already gone above and beyond the call to help her, and she was grateful for all that he had done, but it had to end.

Daisy didn't understand why it hurt so bad if she were doing the right thing. As the tears poured out, she felt empty and hollow. Where there were memories now, those memories had yellow tape around them as if they were a field that had to heal on its own by lying fallow.

Damien didn't have altruistic motives, but in this case, he was right, and that made it worse. It wasn't until it was called off that she realized how many ways she depended on Patrick. Patrick was funny, and he could take and receive a joke. He was a great conversationalist, and he was generally just good company to have around. The best and worst part of it was, Patrick was her friend. They had shared enough that they had inside jokes. Daisy admitted that besides Hannah, she trusted Patrick.

Why couldn't he be a local boy so they would have something in common and things wouldn't be so complicated? Could have, would have, and should have didn't solve a thing. She needed to find a way to get past the initial pain and the consistent throbbing that plagued her even when she was working. She had survived being alone before; she was sure she could survive again.

Daisy entered the shop through the back. She didn't really want to talk to anyone today. She knew Tate was opening the shop, so she didn't need to come in. She wasn't scheduled to come into the shop today, but she thought it was better to go into work rather than stay at home and sulk.

She knew there was a problem when she saw the back door was open. She went in and grabbed a bat that she kept by the door. When she tiptoed into the shop, wanting to make sure a robber wasn't there, she was shocked but for all of the wrong reasons.

Tate stood in the embrace of a young man. He had his hand on her waist and was stroking her hair. Daisy heard the jingle of bells and expected Tate to leave, but she would be disappointed. Instead of leaving, Tate stayed in the young man's embrace.

"Hey, I need to see who is at the front of the store."

The young man laughed and continued to stroke her hair.

"Really, give me ten more minutes. They're here for flowers, so they aren't in a rush."

Daisy understood now more than ever what it meant to have someone like you and wanting to be with them. What she didn't want was that need to take precedence while she was being paid to tend the store. When it was clear that no one was going to go to the front, Daisy decided she had seen enough.

"Good morning," Daisy said as she walked into the room.

At first, Tate didn't respond, and she looked somewhat annoyed until she realized who it was. Daisy could see all of her emotions fly across her face until she finally pushed her boyfriend away.

"Hello, Daisy, you came in."

"I did." She went over to the young man who looked annoyed. His face went from frustrated to happy. "I'm Daisy, the owner."

The young man had brown eyes and an easy smile. "Hello, Daisy. I'm the quarterback, Halloran Towns."

"It's good to meet you, Halloran. I can see that the two of you are wrapping up a conversation that is of the utmost importance, but I'm going to have to worry her from you."

Halloran ran his hand down Tate's side as he was leaving. When he was out the door, Daisy faced Tate. "Do I even have to speak?"

Tate looked longingly at the door before she answered in a sing-song voice. "You're right, I should have told him to meet me at the front."

Daisy looked around and tried to find the calm place in her. In lieu of everything else, this was just one more thing to tip the scale.

"I want to make sure you understand how important it is for you to be in the front of the store manning it. We talked about how we still need a friendly face to help people with their selections."

Tate rolled her eyes and then replied, "We weren't doing anything wrong. If anyone came into the store and they were serious, I made sure to serve anyone who was a serious customer."

"I am listening to you, Tate, but I think you need to listen to me. I don't think you having a boyfriend is appropriate because your young man seems a bit mature and—"

Tate stood up and braced her feet as if she were going to do a jumping jack. "Daisy, I want you to know that I appreciate the job, but this job doesn't get to determine my personal life," she pouted.

Daisy looked at the young woman and felt her hackles go up from such a definitive and aggressive answer.

"You're correct, Tate. What you do on your personal time is yours, but if you are sitting in this backroom here, you are here to work, and that means that I'm paying you. That, in turn, means that when you are in this room, we are on my time. So I get a say in who you are with and what you are doing."

Tate took a step back, and Daisy could see she had expected that exchange to go differently. A lot of jobs in town catered to the young. Daisy was not a part of that thinking, and she was not too proud to chalk this up as a loss and get another worker.

Tate shook her head. "No, no, I really need this."

"I like you, Tate, but I need to know you are reliable."

Tate held up her hand as if she were swearing on a Bible. "I'm reliable. Please, just give me another chance, and I won't let you down."

Daisy thought on it, and her gut kicked in again and said she should go with the other candidate, but she wanted to give Tate a second chance.

"Okay, let's start again. You can man the front, and I'll take care of inventory and orders." She watched Tate go to the front and then she took a breath and went on to try and lose herself in the inventory work.

⚘

Patrick was putting a second coat of paint on the porch railings. It was one of the few things he could do that was mindless and still productive. He was making a plan to see Daisy, but it wasn't completely planned out, and he didn't like to move until his plan was complete. Daisy was too important for him to move impulsively.

He looked up the road and saw the plume of smoke coming down the road. As it got closer, he could see that it was a blue convertible. At first, he thought it was Damien, but it became very apparent that it wasn't when he saw the streaming floral scarf. With a slam of the door, Clarissa strode out in front of the car and made her presence known.

"Hello, Clarissa, to what do I—"

"Just cut the crap, Patrick. We have a problem, and you're too slow to solve it."

Patrick was confused and taken aback when he saw how forceful Clarissa was.

Holding up his hand in a defensive measure, he waited for Clarissa to approach.

"I'm not clear what's going on but—"

Holding up her hand, she stopped him. "I don't have all day to go over things with you. I'm not even sure it would help you if I did. What I want to say to you is you have hurt Daisy's feelings. It seems odd to me that I would have read this relationship wrong. Have you lost interest in Daisy? Was I wrong?"

"No, you weren't wrong. I just need some time to fix some loose ends, and then I'll be able to go back to Daisy."

Clarissa stood there at the bottom of his steps, tapping her shoes to a rhythm that only she could hear.

Patrick put down the paintbrushes and met Clarissa halfway.

"I know she's not happy and I'm working on it. I wanted to make sure I did everything right. I may not get more than one shot, so I want to make sure I do it the right way. It's been hard for us both, but I promise I'm going to do right by her."

Clarissa stared at him for a moment and then took off her shades, closed the space between them, and spoke to him as she poked him in the chest.

"I'm not a patient woman, and I don't like there to be distress in Sweet Blooms that I don't cause. Make it right, or I'll make sure you lose the land and you don't get a dime." With those words, she turned to go back to her car.

"Clarissa, you know you aren't as bad as everyone thinks you are."

She turned, pulled her glasses down, and then looked over the top of them to see Patrick.

"I want you to know I'm twice as bad as everyone thinks. Sweet Blooms is my home, and I care about the people who live here. That doesn't mean I'm soft. It means that I'm possessive. Get it right, city boy."

With those words, she turned on her heel and got in her car. Patrick smiled and thought to himself, *you have to love the women of Sweet Blooms.*

Daisy had just come out of the shower when she heard the knock on the door. The way her day was going, it was probably Damien calling to make sure she knew how inadequate she was. She didn't know if she could really handle another face-off with him. Prepping herself for the worst, she opened the door and saw the last person she expected to see at the door.

"Don't slam the door on me. I need to talk to you."

She couldn't have slammed the door if she wanted to. Daisy was lucky if she was able to put two words together much less move her body. It was Patrick. He looked amazing. His hair was perfect, the timbre of his voice was intoxicating, and as usual, he looked as if he had just stepped off of a movie set.

She had to think about what to do. Were her eyes swollen? Did she look as washed out as she felt? In the middle of the night, she had imagined so many scenarios where she was able to scream her frustrations at him as well as fall into his arms. All of those outcomes left her, and she was left with the picture in front of her. She was faced with the man she had somehow fallen for.

Patrick reached out and ran a finger along her cheek.

"Don't send me away. I came to make it right for us both. I came to fix what's broken because I don't want to lose this thing we have between us."

"What thing?"

"Is that where we are? Are we at the place where we deny the special relationship we have? We're a couple. Like every couple, we have problems. Let's do something new and actually talk about our issues instead of letting our issues run us."

"I need—"

Patrick interrupted her. "I need you. Can I come in? Will you give us a chance?"

Daisy stepped back, and Patrick walked in. The door closed behind him.

"What did he say, Daisy?"

She blinked her eyes and looked at him. "How do you know it was Damien who said anything?"

"I know Damien. He doesn't give up, and he plays dirty when he gets desperate. What did he say? We're too different?"

Daisy laughed. "He said I was too naïve to be with you and you were innately dishonest and couldn't be trusted not to take advantage of me."

He stepped closer to her and cupped her face and then tucked strands of her hair behind her ear. "He doesn't know you. He doesn't know how strong you are. Sweet Blooms isn't always as easy to manage as a city person may think. You have shown me how to be strong without losing myself. You showed me how to look at the world in a whole different way. Don't walk away from me, Daisy."

A person's life could change in minutes. When she woke up this morning, she thought for sure she was going to have to find a way to get through life without Patrick, and now she was practically in his arms.

"Daisy?"

Daisy looked up into his eyes and smiled. She gave him a nod and blinked back the tears of happiness. "If you're willing to work with this country girl, then I'll put in the work."

Patrick laughed. "No problem. I've found that country girls are a lot fiercer than they seem, especially when they are protecting people they care about."

She saw his head bend down, and she closed her eyes as his shadow covered her. His arms circled around her and pulled her into his embrace. Then his lips touched hers, and she was once again swept up in the feeling like a warm breeze that moves through the field. The slow burn started in her stomach and grew like a seedling in the ground. The feeling snaked through her body. His lips brushed against hers, and in a heartbeat, she was swept away in another gale of feeling and safety.

When he drew back and looked into her eyes, she saw the question in his eyes even before he asked. "Does this mean that you are giving us a go?" he asked.

She stared into his eyes and then wrapped her hand around his neck, pulling him back down for a second kiss.

"I want you to know that I was sure this time."

Then he leaned down and kissed her again. This time the kiss was done through their laughter.

Daisy pulled back. "So I guess we're a couple now, with our first fight out of the way."

"I wasn't sure how it was going to go, but if you'd like, I know a nice café in town that I can take you to."

"Really?" she said with a smile.

"Yes, I do know a place, and I think you'll like it."

He led her to his car, and he took her to the café to celebrate their first fight and makeup.

Seventeen

"I'm glad you found your way, Mr. Tyler," Clarissa said from her seat at the table. The afternoon breeze offered a small relief from the heat.

"How could I refuse a beautiful woman inviting me to lunch," Damien said. Clarissa couldn't believe how thick he was laying it on. She didn't want anything from him; in fact, it was about to be the opposite. She would offer him something instead.

"It's true, I very rarely get turned down, Mr. Tyler, and let's hope you don't fall into that category today," Clarissa said to Damien.

"I have to admit you have my interest," he said. "I didn't think our meeting was left on anything that I could remotely call good footing."

The waitress came by, and Clarissa gave her order. When Damien got ready to give his order, Clarissa held up her hand and told the waitress that he wouldn't be here long enough to have a beverage.

"Okay, you bring me out here, and then you say I won't be here long. What gives here, Clarissa?"

"Damien," Clarissa said. "The reason I've asked you to come here today is because this is where our relationship started and I laid out the guidelines to being in Sweet Blooms. I think that it's only fitting that wherever I started, it would be the place that we bring our business to a conclusion."

The waitress came back and gave Clarissa her order, a tall lemonade.

"When we last met one another, you told me there was some concern that people you were dealing with would come to Sweet Blooms and possibly do some harm to Daisy and maybe to some other members of Sweet Blooms."

"Please, please, let's not go over what might have been hasty words. I want to do all I can to help wrap up this situation."

Clarissa looked at Damien, and it became clear how someone could wish another bodily harm.

"Tell me, Damien, what was the price you were looking for in regards to the land?"

She saw his eyes light up with greed, and for a moment, Clarissa was tempted to just get up and leave him at the table. Hannah had been seen with a smiling Daisy the other day, and they were both bubbling about the men in their lives. Clarissa knew that whatever it was that Patrick had done had worked, and all was well with them. To Clarissa's mind, that left Damien a loose end.

When she woke this morning, she needed to make sure she was in control, so she wore her royal purple dress. It had no sleeves, and it was a button-down dress. She had matching low flats on with the dress, and as usual, she had swept her hair up into a messy knot. After much deliberation, she had decided no one cared about her hair, or at least they wouldn't care once they understood what it was she had done. She was brought out of her haze when Damien started to ramble on and on about how he worked with other agencies, and he knew that he would be able to deliver some much-needed reports as well as run some old reports.

"I knew the way was through the board. I want to thank you so much for getting me an audience with the board. From there I will be able to—"

Clarissa held up her hand. "I didn't say I got you an audience with the board. What I said was, how much money did you want for the land?"

She could almost see him spending the money before it ever hit his hand. When he gave a figure, she immediately haggled with him and asked for another number. After about twenty minutes of going back and forth, they had a number that both of them agreed on.

Rubbing his hands, he looked at Clarissa as she sipped her tea.

"I'm good with the number. When are we going to go before the board?"

"To be honest, Mr. Tyler, the board wants to have nothing to do with you. They are very content to let this drag out for however long it may take. On the other hand, I will offer you a one time deal."

The look of suspicion took up residence on Damien's face.

"If you aren't here for the board, who are you representing?"

Clarissa smiled. "I represent the best interests for Sweet Blooms." With that out of the way, she reached into her purse and pulled out a check and wrote the agreed upon amount. "Take this money and go away."

When she was done filling out the check, she handed it to Damien.

"This is the money you wanted and the amount that is required. Now the only thing you need to do is to pack your gear and get out of town."

Damien looked at the check and then back at Clarissa. Before he could speak, he looked back at her.

"Mr. Tyler, don't even think about asking for more money or I'll have your case brought before the board, and if they have their way, you won't ever solve this issue, and then the land will go to them, and they won't have to spend a dime."

Damien reached out and took the check. Sighing, he looked around the afternoon crowd. He wanted to go back to what he knew. Country life might be for some, but it wasn't for him.

"Thank you for doing business with me."

Clarissa watched him leave and then took another sip of her tea. She couldn't do a lot with her current situation, but when she could do something about it, she would.

<h1 style="text-align:center">Epilogue</h1>

Bain Parcels was glad to be home. He wanted to be able to come to Adam's wedding. He was Adam's best man, and he was honored to be here. Bain didn't know what he expected, but what he didn't expect was to walk into Sweet Blooms and find a majority if not all of the people and the feel of the town the same. Sitting in his car outside of the Sweet Blooms Café brought back memories.

Bain Parcels wasn't a household name. He hadn't been a popular person in school. Now women noticed him all the time. Bain knew the price that came with being a top model was the lack of privacy. In truth, most of the time Bain had no problem with reporters, fans, or die-hard fans that threw themselves at him. All of these things he could deal with with no issue at all. There was only one person he couldn't talk to, and she wasn't moved by anything but money.

He knew it wasn't going to be long before she knew he was in town. He didn't know what to expect from her, but he knew it was time. If this wedding had shown him anything, it had shown him that they had been separated too long and they needed to fix what was broken.

All in all, Bain Parcels wanted his wife back, and she had better get ready for an all-out assault from what the tabloids were calling the sexiest man out there.

He reached into his pocket and pulled out his wallet. When he opened it up, he was greeted by the photo that he had kept of their wedding day. No matter where he went, he kept the photo with him. It was a little worse for wear. The photo had a couple more creases in it than he would have liked, but his wife looked just as beautiful now as she did then.

As if he had beckoned her from thin air, Bain looked up and, walking down the street, he saw his one and only wife coming his way. He got out of the car and smiled.

"Good morning, Clarissa. We need to talk."

I hope you enjoyed Patrick and Daisy's story. Check out book eight in the Love Happen Series *Sweet Healing* and read Bain and Clarissa's story.

Sign up to my newsletter to receive updates on new releases, sale promotions, and free books.

susanwarnerauthor.com

www.ingramcontent.com/pod-product-compliance
Lightning Source LLC
Chambersburg PA
CBHW071827190726
48292CB00005B/1646